# THE ORPHAN DAUGHTER OF LUPIN LANE

## A HISTORICAL VICTORIAN SAGA

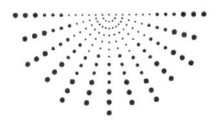

### DOLLY PRICE

Publisher's Note: This is a work of fiction. Names, characters, places, and incidents are a product of the author's imagination. Locales and public names are sometimes used for atmospheric purposes. Any resemblance to actual people, living or dead, or to businesses, companies, events, institutions, or locales is completely coincidental.

© 2019 PUREREAD LTD

PUREREAD.COM

CONTENTS

*Introduction* v

| | |
|---|---:|
| Chapter 1 | 1 |
| Chapter 2 | 8 |
| Chapter 3 | 17 |
| Chapter 4 | 21 |
| Chapter 5 | 26 |
| Chapter 6 | 34 |
| Chapter 7 | 38 |
| Chapter 8 | 41 |
| Chapter 9 | 50 |
| Chapter 10 | 55 |
| Chapter 11 | 64 |
| Chapter 12 | 74 |
| Chapter 13 | 78 |
| Chapter 14 | 86 |
| Chapter 15 | 93 |
| Chapter 16 | 98 |
| Chapter 17 | 101 |
| Chapter 18 | 104 |
| Chapter 19 | 109 |
| Chapter 20 | 112 |
| Chapter 21 | 115 |
| Chapter 22 | 118 |
| Chapter 23 | 121 |
| Chapter 24 | 124 |
| Chapter 25 | 130 |
| Chapter 26 | 136 |
| Chapter 27 | 140 |
| Chapter 28 | 152 |
| Chapter 29 | 154 |

| | |
|---|---|
| Chapter 30 | 161 |
| Chapter 31 | 166 |
| Chapter 32 | 171 |
| *Our Gift To You* | 175 |

INTRODUCTION

A PERSONAL WORD FROM PUREREAD

> Dear reader,
>
> It is our utmost pleasure and privilege to bring these wonderful stories to you. I am so very proud of our amazing team of writers, and the delight they continually bring to us all with their beautiful tales of hope, faith, courage and love.
>
> Only once a story is read does it fulfill it's God given purpose, and that makes you, the dear reader, the key that unlocks the treasures that lay within the pages of this book.
>
> *Thank you for choosing PureRead!*

**A Warm Welcome From Dolly Price**

# PureRead
## Clean Reads
## For Pure Hearts

*To find out more about PureRead and receive new release information and other goodies from Dolly Price go to our website*
*PureRead.com/dollyprice*

* * *

**Enjoy The Story!**

CHAPTER ONE

James Coll was used to seeing children pressing their noses against the bow window of his little bakery, but this little dark-haired girl had been lingering there for quite a while now. Only the top of her head and her eyes were visible to him, and those two large dark eyes were casting anxious glances at him, and in the last minutes, seemed to have acquired a desperation. She was hungry, he supposed, like many children in the East End. He'd go and give her a penny bun that was left on the shelf. It was time to close the bakery anyhow; this dark afternoon in late November was seeing a cold, heavy rain come down with the night, and across the narrow lane Mr. Shipman, the cobbler, was letting down his blind. Gaslights lit the windows of the other houses, all homes. Jim came out from behind the counter with a bun in his hand and opened the bakery door.

Lupin Lane was the dark, narrow end of Lupin Street, Whitechapel, distinguished from its wider partner by houses much older and smaller. It had six houses on either side, all stonecut two-storeys built as cottages several hundred years before, when the area had been a village. Now they had an old tottering look. It had had a blind end before 1800, when the blind end was opened and a wider street, with buildings more fitting for a city, was built. This extension was marked with an archway to give the entrance a more pleasing look, but at night, those approaching Lupin Lane from Lupin Street were afraid to pass under it for fear of criminals lurking in its shadows. The street housed a public-house called The Foremast, and the Arch was a place the patrons feared to pass upon leaving late at night if they had quarrelled with another patron.

Lupin Lane was almost too narrow for the carts and cabs not wanting to go around to High Street by a longer way, and as was usual for this time on a winter evening, they squeezed by one after another in steady procession. The archway was etched black as coal, the wet cobbles under it shining from the light of the streetlamp nearby.

"Well, little Miss, isn't it time you were getting along 'ome now?" Mr. Coll asked the little girl, gently pulling her by the arm out of the path of an oncoming water cart which promised to leave very little room between it and his bakery window.

She looked warily at him, but her eyes, black as coal, wide and hopeful, wandered to the bread. He held it out, and she took it in her small grubby hands and ate it eagerly.

"Where do you live, little Miss?" he asked. He knew most of the children in the neighbourhood, and this little one he did not remember seeing before. He did not trust the girl to the mercy of these dark streets and the rogues that would be soon about; many making their way to the Foremast. He would be uneasy until he knew she was safely home. Was she from one of the new tenements that had sprung up near the Waste? He might have to take her hand and bring her to her door.

"The Heath," was her reply, in a whisper.

"The Heath!" he replied. But as to which one, she couldn't answer.

The bakery door opened and his wife Sophie joined him, pulling her shawl over her head.

"She must be lost, Jim! And frozen to death, no coat! It's about to pour down. What's your name, luv?" she asked with tenderness.

"Isabella," said the girl in a low voice.

"And what age are you, Isabella?"

"Four."

"Where are your mama and papa?" was her next question.

The little girl's face dropped in sorrow, and she seemed about to burst into tears.

"Mama was on the ship."

"And Papa?"

"Papa was very cross."

They digested this odd conjunction of facts, but concluded that something dreadful had happened between Mama and Papa, and that there was nothing helpful in the information.

"Bring 'er in, Jim, and warm her up. Somebody must be looking for her."

"I was thinking that thought exactly," Jim said. He and Sophie had a very soft heart for children. It was a great sorrow to them—but mostly to the motherly woman—that after fifteen years of marriage, they had no children of their own.

Sophie was a good-looking woman of thirty-four. Her hair, which she normally tucked under a cap, was still a strong shade of auburn, and more often than not little curls escaped to her forehead. A round and rosy face, with dimpled cheeks, gave her a benevolent expression, and this was enhanced by the kindness in her bright, keen eyes. She was a little plump but carried herself well. Her dress, after countless washings down through the years, was now a dull version of its original emerald; she wore a white apron over it; and her shawl, an old brown woolen thing, was darned here and there.

Sophie took the little girl's hand, remarking on how cold it was, and brought her inside, past the bakery into the room beyond, a small, warm living room bathed in a golden glow by the oil lamp. A white-painted dresser, laden with everyday pottery and Willow pattern china, almost filled one wall. The chintz sofa under the window had seen better days. Filling the centre of the room was the table, now enveloped in a scarlet gingham cloth, and laid for supper. She lifted Isabella into one of the two deal armchairs by the open range, their only concession to luxury being a flat cushion on each seat.

Molly, the maid-of-all-work, looked up from cutting bread at the table. Sophie asked her to warm some milk.

"This little lamb is lost. Do you know her, Molly? Have you ever seen her about?"

"She's not from around 'ere, ma'am," said Molly with conviction. "I'd say I know every face 'round here."

"So Isabella," Sophie said gently as the little girl drained the milk a few minutes later, "Tell me everything that happened you today."

But the empty cup was tumbling from Isabella's hand, falling to the hearthrug, as the child's eyelids drooped, and her head fell on her neck in sudden, exhausted sleep.

Sophie picked her up and laid her on the sofa. She was not well nourished, she thought, thin little legs encased in black stockings, her blue dress fraying here and there, the hem drooping in the front, but she wore good, stout boots. Her pinafore was dirty and torn. Strands of damp jet-black hair were plastered around her face, which was none too clean. Sophie took a towel and gently dried her hair, then wiped a dark streak of what looked like soot from her cheek. Taking up her hand, she saw that her fingernails were not only dirty, but that there appeared to be dark red spots streaked under them.

"Bring the lamp close, Molly!"

"Yes, ma'am. Look at the thin arms of her, sure God love her!"

Sophie lifted one limp hand close to the lamp and extended the fingers.

"Do you see the colour of that dirt under her nails? What do you think is under them, Molly?"

"Well ma'am, if I was asked in a Court of Law, I would swear, that those rusty stains there was blood! She fought somebody, somebody tryin' to do 'er harm I'm sure—scratched 'im to ribbons I hope!"

CHAPTER TWO

"The poor little mite doesn't know anything about herself, except for a ship. She talks about the ship."

Sophie was in the bakery, chatting to her neighbour, Mrs. Smith.

"Maybe 'er muvver drowned then," offered Mrs. Smith. "And she said 'er fovver was angry? Maybe—" she dropped her voice even though nobody else was in the bakery, and wagged one bony finger. "This is wot 'appened, Mrs. Coll, the fovver go' angry with the muvver on the ship—and pushed 'er over the side. The child saw it 'appen! She won't talk of it, little mite!"

"But how would Isabella get ashore?" Sophie frowned, doubting Mrs. Smith's version. Everybody knew she was partial to stories of high drama and got her son to read one out to her every week from a periodical he brought home, discarded by his employer.

"The child run from 'im, she's afraid of 'im! Soon's they come ashore, she run as fast as she can up from the docks there. Then she got 'ungry and the smell of bread made her stop 'ere! That's wot 'appened, I will bet my life on it!"

"She has neither hat nor cloak—"

"She run from 'im from the boardin' 'ouse then! You should go down to the docks, Sophie, and make inquiries."

Sophie shifted her feet.

"Now don't get too attached to 'er," warned her friend, "because there'll be an a grandfovver, or an aunt, or somebody, comin' to fetch 'er, once they work out what 'appened on the ship, they'll have the fovver arrested, and 'e will be hung, and then of course they will want the child, in place of the muvver that was pushed overboard. Like in the story *'Muvver's 'Eartbreak'*. This woman, Lady Pe'ifogg, got attached to an orphan she took in, only to 'ave her taken away by a relative. I cried my eyes out when Ned read it out. I'm so lucky to 'ave Ned read to me."

Jim returned then, for he had been out on a late delivery. He looked with his usual mild, indulgent suspicion at Mrs. Smith, and that lady nodded to him and departed, pulling her shawl around her, muttering *'muvver's 'eartbreak'*.

"Did she ask for credit?"

"No, not this time."

"Good, 'cos she doesn't need it. She has two sons now at the Ironworks."

"But Mrs. Foster was in. I gave her a quartern loaf on credit."

"Oh that's orright. Poor woman, hard cheese to be left with five young 'uns."

"Sometimes, Jim, I have thought that all the hungry children in the neighbourhood are ours *in a way*, as we give out so much without expecting to be paid. Did God keep us childless, because we were to look after the poor ones?" Poor Sophie mused all the time as to why she, who so longed for a houseful of little ones, had not been granted the blessing, and this was her latest theory.

"We don't know the ways of God," Jim replied, checking the stock book. "All I know is that people what has enough, has to give. I don't think a lot on those things as much as you, Sophie. We never go hungry ourselves. Do we want for anything, Sophie?"

"No, not at all," Sophie said with haste. She had fallen in love with Jim, not just because of the sincere look in his deep blue eyes, but because he was kind, gentle, and God-fearing. His humble and charitable heart endeared him to her. Coll's Bakery was a small, plain affair, but hard work. And though she might occasionally look with interest at a fancy hat in a shop window when she visited her mother in Cheapside, she found it always in her heart to thank God that they were able to help others, and that Jim was generous as he could be to her also, for any extra money she asked for, she received without question. His own needs were very simple—give him his eel pie'n mash, or any other good dinner, his roast beef of a Sunday and his pipe—and he was happy as Larry. The life of a baker was a rough one. He slept between seven o'clock in the evening and eleven, then it was up to make the dough. He napped while it rose, then the kneading began, and so his day. They could not afford an apprentice, not yet. She got up to help him knead sometimes, four feet pounding the dough in the trough was a lot faster than two!

They were better off than most in the neighbourhood.

Whitechapel was one of the areas of London near the busy docklands, where many people lived hand to mouth. It was common for one family—and sometimes two—to live in one squalid room in one of the many tenements that sprang up to house the throngs that settled there. Work on the docks or the other industries related to shipping could be irregular. Many people lived from day to day, eating if the men found work, going without if they did not. There were widows who scavenged in rubbish, orphans absorbed into crime gangs, homeless women who sold themselves for the price of a bed in a doss-house, and newborn babies carried to the Foundling Hospital after dark when nobody was about.

Jim Coll had lived here all his life. He was a part of Whitechapel. Not everybody could work, not every man had his health, or a trade. Many people lived one step away from starvation, and he kept day-old bread for them, half-price. He even gave it away sometimes.

The East End was Jim's world; if he as much as crossed London Bridge, he was homesick.

"Has there been anybody by about the little girl?" he asked.

"Not a soul. Nobody around here has ever seen her before. Jim, now that you're back, I must go and see if she is orright. Molly's sitting with her."

Sophie hurried out the door leading to the narrow hallway, from where a staircase led to two rooms upstairs. She opened the door of the smallest room, thinking it was very dark and gloomy for a child to wake up in—she should put up nice curtains, with bright flowers, or butterflies. Isabella was sleeping, her new doll in her arms.

Molly reported that she hadn't stirred. "I'll see if her clothes are dry, ma'am, they should be, or very nearly, hangin' up all day over the fire. I'll run the flatiron over 'em to give 'em extra."

Sophie had asked Jim for a few shillings that morning and gone to the market. She'd bought a girls' nightgown—in good condition and clean—from the *Old Clothes Good As New* shop, and saw the doll on her way home on Charlie's *Fancy Ware* stall, sitting between a set of old china and a brown clock. She was almost new! She had long dark hair like Isabella, with a big white bow, and long-lashed soft brown eyes. She wore a purple dress with a white pinafore with big pockets.

As Sophie gazed on her, Isabella awoke. Her eyes wandered with confusion around the room, as if she had trouble remembering, and finally rested on Sophie, who had withdrawn a little so as not to frighten her.

The child sat up and cried straightaway, and Sophie held her close, and with many 'poor dears' and 'poor little pets' told her she was safe, and encouraged her to look at her new doll and to name her. Through great sobs, the doll was eventually named Maria. The child sobbed for a time about someone named Vovó, which Sophie thought must be a nickname for a favourite aunt, and mentioned again about the ship, looking up at a man on a horse, and a man taking her away, and another ship, and being sick over somebody's—Sophie didn't catch the name—gown, so Sophie quite lost track. Isabella came back to Vovó again and again, mentioned again that papa was very cross, and added that the old lady scared her, and there was a monster on the wall. When she was calm, Sophie wrapped a warm woolen shawl about her, carried her downstairs, sat her at the table on a chair to which two large cushions had been added for height, where to her delight she drank all her milk and ate all her bread and jam.

Isabella looked about at these strange, but kind people. She did not know where she was, and what happened yesterday still troubled her, but for now, she felt safe. Would papa come and get her? She was not sure that she wished him to. The man who sat at the table was not like her papa. He smelled like bread, and smiled down at her as he cut up her bread in little pieces, and she felt his gentleness and stared up at him with a great deal of gratitude and wonder. The lady was not as beautiful as Mama, but she was very loving to her, like Vovó. They were old, but Molly was young, with a bright smile, and she liked Molly too.

But Isabella did not know what was to become of her, so she asked, in a very small and timid voice, "Will I stay here now?"

"You may stay as long as you wish, Isabella," said the kind lady, cutting an apple tart Molly had taken from the oven.

The man stirred his tea, and looking at her, smiled again.

"Can Vovó come too?"

"Who is Vovó, dearest?" smiled the lady across the table.

"She lives in town. She visits us in the Heath."

"Have you ever been to Vovó's house?" asked the man.

"Yesterday, I was."

"Do you know where it is, Isabella?"

"In town."

"What's Vovó's real name, Isabella?"

"Vovó is her real name!" Isabella's lip trembled, how could people not understand? But the lady was beside her immediately, and embraced her, and said that everything would be all right. Would she like more bread and jam? She was not to worry. They would find Vovó.

CHAPTER THREE

A week slipped by. The little girl appeared to be content, but woke in the night with nightmares. Sophie decided to put her to bed on the sofa, and when Jim came down at eleven, she carried her upstairs and put her in their own bed, and as she retired also at that time, if Isabella—or Bella as they had begun to call her—woke up screaming, she would be there to console her.

In any case, the smaller room by rights belonged to Sophie's mother, who came to stay very often. She had been widowed five years. The late Mr. Clancy had been a senior clerk in a law firm, and Sophie had, as a girl growing up in Cheapside, had a better standard of living than the one she had now.

"I thought I should come and see you, Sophie, since you neglected to write to me," Mrs. Clancy called out as she let herself in the street door that led, through the dark narrow hall, directly to the living room. She put her head inside the inner door. "Who's this little one? A neighbour's child, is she? What would your neighbours do, without you to mind their children while the mothers gallivant around Whitechapel? I hope they appreciate you. I haven't seen this one before."

Her gaze lingered upon Bella, who was sitting at the table drawing on the back of a piece of old wallpaper left over from a papering.

"Oh Mother, it's good to see you! But hush, don't frighten the little thing," was her daughter's response.

"Frighten her! When did I ever frighten a child? Are you going to ask me to take off my hat and cloak, or not? I got drenched."

"Of course, Mother, I am very sorry—I will tell you all, and I didn't mean for to offend, it's just that Bella is very"—she dropped her voice—"nervous. She's a foundling left in the street, had a terrible tragedy, her mother lost at sea, her father—well, I don't know —" Sophie gave the history in a hushed, hurried voice as she hung her mother's cloak by the fire and put her sitting down with a hot cup of tea and a buttered scone.

Mrs. Clancy was completely amazed. They spoke in whispers, so that Bella, completely absorbed in her drawing, her little feet swinging to and fro under the table, could not hear them.

Sophie's mother was a woman of medium height, still handsome, and looked younger than her fifty-five years. Her husband had been a careful manager and left her the house clear of mortgage, and she also had an Annuity. She had sold the house and together with other widows in her situation now boarded at a respectable house in Cheapside. She was very happy with the arrangement, had no responsibilities, and was free to go about as she wished. She dressed better than her daughter. She had been of the opinion that Sophie could have done a lot better for herself than James Coll. However, the years had softened her view of him, mostly because the young man she had wanted Sophie to marry had turned out to be a gambler, and his wife had to go out charring. Sophie had chosen right. Mrs. Clancy was now very fond of her son-in-law, though she wished he would bring in more money so that her daughter could be better dressed, but she respected that he never adulterated the bread. Seeing that they were generous to the poor, Mrs. Clancy was generous to Sophie and Jim.

She listened to Sophie's story with an open mind, but lost no time in finding that Sophie regarded the child as *theirs*, already. She had to caution her. But it was time for supper, and Jim had closed the bakery. She had brought some cold bacon and apples, as she was unexpected. She noticed that the child was very quiet, though. When she asked her to show her what she had drawn, Isabella showed her a stick outline of a sea vessel, and two stick figures, both women, one thin with long wavy hair in thick bold strokes, the other with a big bun on her head, both smiling broadly. She was going to ask her who they were, but a look from her daughter made her keep her mouth closed. Soon, Bella was put into her nightgown and went to sleep on the sofa cocooned in warm blankets, with a pillow under her head, and Jim went up to bed before his night's work. Now she could say what was on her mind to Sophie, and she could hardly keep it in any longer!

CHAPTER FOUR

When Molly had gone home, Mrs. Clancy launched her thoughts into the open.

"Mind you don't get hurt, Sophie. Somebody will come someday and take her home. Somebody is looking for her, at this minute, I warrant."

"Jim has scoured the newspapers, Mother. There's nothing about a missing child with her name and description. He went to the police, they have no reports. He went to Reverend Morton; he said that if he heard anything, he would come to tell us. There's nobody looking for her, Mother, because her mother drowned and her father—maybe he's in foreign parts."

"You should be continually asking her about what happened, about how she came to be here."

"Mother, she has a very confusing story—she's only four years old! Barely old enough to know her name and age!"

"It's you I'm thinking of, Sophie, as well as the child."

"Are you afraid of—?" Sophie asked, a little accusingly.

"There's nothing I'd like better for you than to have a child—I have prayed and prayed—"

"Oh Mother, I know!" Sophie was contrite.

"If she becomes yours, Sophie, I should be very happy to call Bella my grandchild. As for adoption, I don't suppose there'd be any suspicions this time—"

"It's nothing like the time we made the attempt, Mother." Sophie felt herself shivering in spite of the fire.

Neither liked to recall the memory. Seven years before, Sophie and Jim had placed an advertisement in the newspaper, as was common, stating that they wished to adopt a child. What had happened next had been very disturbing. Instead of replies, the police pounced, and demanded she produce the two other children she had adopted, which of course they had never done. They searched the house before they realised they had the wrong person. They were looking for a woman who frequently advertised herself, under different names, as a woman wanting to adopt, and asked for money from natural mothers for the child's initial expenses. That procured, this woman was suspected of disposing of the unfortunate baby, either selling the infant or worse, and beginning again after a few months with another advertisement.

Sophie and Jim, and Sophie's mother, had been very shaken by the experience. Sophie had not attempted another adoption. She heard later that a woman was caught, charged, and punished. How could people treat infants with such callousness? It was beyond her understanding.

"There's nothing to fear, Mother. Perhaps Isabella has been given to us, in a way. I'm going to put that other time out of my head."

"You're attached already, I can see that. Well it's your business, and I shan't interfere. I only want what's best for you. Why didn't you want me to ask her who it was she drew?"

"Because we've decided that she should forget. The ship is on her mind. She wakes up screaming about a ship, and about a man who took her, and a monster on a wall—if you only heard her, Mother! It would break your heart. We think that if nobody comes to claim her, she should forget all her past, and begin again—with us. We're not going to encourage her to remember. It causes her too much pain. Would you like to help me with some sewing? I bought some cotton flannel, this apple green and a plaid, for two little dresses, and a good red wool for Sundays, but she needs pinafores and underthings. I'll turn up the lamp."

"Of course, dear. Remember, you have to make her clothes big! Children outgrow everything in a short time! If it's not a delicate question, have you enough money for this?"

"Mother, we have a bit put by, and meant to use it for an apprentice, but we'll put off the apprentice for a while. Oh, look, she's stirring."

Sophie stood and watched the little figure for the signs she now knew well, the restlessness, the thrashing of limbs, the clawing of the air, as if she were caught in a net, trying to get away. Bella's face puckered and her voice rose in a shrill scream. Sophie had bent to her and held her instantly, waking her gently with soothing words, until she calmed, realised where she was and who she was with, and settled down again, Maria tucked in her arms.

Mrs. Clancy had witnessed the sad nightmare for herself, and heard the cries, and tears had started to her eyes. She was completely in agreement with her daughter that it would be much better for Bella's memories not to be encouraged at all, but to be left to fade away.

CHAPTER FIVE

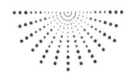

Nearly every child in Lupin Lane and half of those on Lupin Street knew Isabella within two weeks of her arrival. The first few made friends with her on her third day, as soon as she appeared on the street, doll in one hand, Sophie holding the other, as they walked to Whitechapel High Street. Sophie had had to coax her out of the house. The child seemed afraid to leave her place of safety. The best way to deal with a fear was to face it. Sophie stopped and introduced her to every little girl she knew. The doll attracted admiration, and soon after, there were bold knocks on the street door to see if Bella would come out to play. Bella seemed willing, but afraid, to leave the safety of the house without Sophie, so she went with her at first, watching her while the little ones played and ran about. She soon lost her fear of being outside.

The Mitchell family lived all in one room on the ground floor of Jerome's Buildings in an alley off High Street, and Gracie, about the same age as Bella, soon became a constant companion. Her mother would not allow her to go anywhere on her own, so she enlisted her big brother Philip to bring her to the Colls' door.

Bella was popular; she liked to have friends, and was nice to everybody. There was no doubt in the mind of any younger child that the Colls were Bella's mamma and papa, and one morning shortly before Christmas Sophie heard young Gracie Mitchell, slight in form, with fair wispy hair and an adorable lisp, ask: "Bella, will your mamma bake gingerbread for uth at Chrithmas?"

Bella did not know the answer, and to Sophie's delight, she turned her eyes up to her in questioning.

"Will you bake gingerbread at Chrithmas, Mth. Coll?" repeated Gracie with eagerness. "Mamma seth you will."

"Your mamma is right, Gracie, I will!" Sophie said, and saw a smile spread across Bella's face.

After that, Bella, who had called her nothing up to then, and Sophie not wanting to push the matter, began of her own volition to call her 'Mamma'. It was music to Sophie's ears, and of course, Jim soon became 'Papa'.

The Sunday before Christmas was the day Mrs. Coll always gave her party for the children of the neighbourhood. She had done this for years now. The living-room was festooned with evergreen boughs and red-berried holly. Sophie and Molly had been busy all Saturday baking gingerbread. Bella had helped. They found her a good little assistant as she ran forwards and backwards with wooden spoons, measures, and the lighter weights—everything unbreakable that they required. She even dragged over, unasked, a bag of brown sugar almost as big as herself. And, for the first time since she had been found, her face lit up with happiness. Isabella giggled out loud, and Sophie exulted as if her own baby had taken her first steps.

The children began to arrive at three o'clock. Gracie was first, as usual accompanied by her older brother Philip, a lanky red-haired lad of eleven, who usually regarded this escorting of his sister a chore, but today, he would be amply compensated by eating a great deal of gingerbread. He would make himself an unofficial adult of the party, on a par with Mr. and Mrs. Coll and Molly O'Brien. He would help with the children, keep them in order, spot the greedy ones stuffing their pockets, break up fights, and eat. This was his bold intention, but it turned out very differently. He was summoned into the bakery by Jim Coll. He was shown the ovens, the furnaces, the long table, the dough-trough, and even the flour bags and the contents of the shelves.

"The yeast comes from Holland. I prefer ale-yeast but I can never get enough. What I bake here is called Household bread in the trade. I don't go in for confectionery, you know, cakes and such."

Philip was politely pretending interest, but all the time worrying if the pile of gingerbread in the kitchen was getting smaller and smaller.

"You're still in school?" asked Mr. Coll.

"Until I'm twelve, sir. That's enough learnin', me Ma says; me Ma wants me to work."

"Has she anything in mind?"

"No, only Da says he doesn't want me in the Ironworks'. The doctor says he has a bad lung from breathin' in—dust or somethin'; and Mr. Tenney got blinded."

"That's hard cheese orright. Do you know that this bakery has been in my family since the sixteenth century?"

"No, sir. That's a long time, sir."

"London was a different place then; Whitechapel had fields. London is really a collection of villages, did you know that?"

"No, sir. I never knew that! Green fields around here, sir! I wish I knew more! The Master—" he halted suddenly.

"Go on, the Master—"

"—visited my mother sir, and asked her was there any way I could stay in school for a few more years—said I was very bright, sir. I was a monitor, sir." Philip lowered his head to hide his flushed face.

"I've noticed you're quick on the uptake."

"Thank you, sir. My mother had to tell the Master no. She was very sorry about it an' all. Mr. Sharp told me then, one day after school was let out, that I should never stop readin', sir. He said—Charles Dickens didn't get schoolin', and that gave me hope of betterin' myself someday, sir. He said I should go in for an occupation where I have to do accounting and the like."

"And do you like reading?"

"I do sir, every book I can lay my hands on, to be honest, I go to a quiet place, up by the Waste; there's a quiet spot, away from all my sisters and the neighbours, so noisy they are, sir. They'd laugh anyway to see me readin', or trying to solve an equation."

"Philip, I have something I want you to think about. I'm looking for an apprentice next year. Baking's a very valuable skill. There'd be plenty of account-keeping. You'd have to work at night, though, to have the bread baked in the early morning, then you have to sell all day, but I manage it orright, sleepin' about five hours in the evening. There are a few hours at night, when you're waitin' for the dough to rise, when you can sack out, or read, or do your equations, whatever you prefer."

Philip did not have to think. "I'm sure I would like it very much, sir. Much better than the Ironworks. Thank you sir."

"Just think about it, Philip, for now. No need to make up your mind for a few months. You can come into the bakery if you like, after school, to see how you like it. I'll pay you a few shillings, for that, and once you get to know the run of it, I can leave you here on your own sometimes."

"Yes, sir, I'd be glad to, sir!" The prospect of jingling money in his pocket was appealing to him, though he knew his mother would get all but a few pennies.

"And as soon as you get your Master Baker's, you'll be free to open up your own business, or become a Journeyman. You'll be master of your own future. If you work hard and learn."

Philip felt very gratified, singled out for this honour by Mr. Coll, who nobody had a bad word to say about. He had no idea if he wanted to become a Master Baker. His thought was that he could eat as much as he liked of the goods, which you couldn't do in the Ironworks. He had to learn a trade, and by the time he was skilled, his father could perhaps stop work. Even now he was frequently unwell. Philip would be grateful to learn a trade. You could make a living with a trade. Even a good living. His mother said so. His father had had to go to work at his age making ship-rope and would have loved the chance to train as a cobbler or a coachmaker, maybe even a baker. Philip felt like a grown-up man.

The door burst open from the kitchen, increasing the noise level suddenly to a deafening roar.

"Mr. Coll!" shouted his wife over the noise, with some mock severity. "Why are you keeping Philip from his gingerbread? The children have made such inroads, if you don't let him go, he won't get any at all!"

"Philip is too old to sit with that crowd of dustbin lids—" began his would-be employer, as Philip thanked him profusely, became a boy again, and hied it to the shrinking pile of gingerbread men and animals in the Tower of Babel.

"Well, what did he say?" asked Mrs. Coll with eagerness, shutting the door behind her.

"He's thinking it over, but I'd say his parents will make the decision. A good, solid lad, I always thought. He's leaving school soon. But I had to leave even earlier to learn the trade."

"I never went at all, as you know." his wife said. "I can teach Isabella her letters at home, as Mother taught me."

CHAPTER SIX

Christmas was approaching, and carol singers were heard in the streets. Mrs. Clancy, having gone to her own home for a few weeks, appeared again to stay the Christmas season, and brought a plucked, cleaned goose. This was a tradition. On December 24$^{th}$, Mr. Coll closed the bakery at six o'clock, but did not come back to the living room as he usually did; instead, he took his hat and coat from the hallstand and went out.

"Where's Papa?" asked Bella.

"He has gone to the market, and won't be long, I promise," said Sophie with cheer. The aroma of mince pies wafted about the room. The goose sat on the blue, Willow-pattern platter in the cold hallway, ready to be roasted in the morning. The cat was confined to the kitchen. They'd had a cat since last week. A stray, like Bella, only the worst for wear, for its ear was torn. Bella was invited to choose its name. She was dissuaded from *Gracie Mitchell*, the name of her best friend, and after much thought decided upon *Tufty Smith*, which was acceptable to everybody, except the Smith was dropped, as she was told the cat had to be a *Coll* like everybody else in the house, or else Mrs. Smith might think she owned Tufty.

"A biddable child, that," remarked Mrs. Clancy. "Good-humoured, isn't she? But is Bella a Coll now?"

"The name she came with—Woodstone, or Westing, or something like that, she told us—is forgotten. I'm not sure she knew what it was, herself. Anyhow, she's a Coll. She's ours. Isabella Coll."

"Here's Papa!" cried Bella, who had a keen ear. She darted out to the hallway, and stopped in amazement, for her Papa was half-dragging, half-carrying a tree inside the door!

"Christmas tree!" she cried in delight. "Are we to have a Christmas tree, Papa?"

"Mind the goose, Jim!" called Sophie, as the limbs swished past the bird, almost knocking it from the platter. The tree was not the only danger for tomorrow's dinner, Tufty had escaped from the kitchen and was licking the skin, artfully dodging the boughs as they brushed past, bent on removing a delicacy for himself, if possible, before the inevitable discovery of his crime. He worked with top speed and efficiency, as practiced in the alleys since the age of seven weeks, and he had almost managed to gnaw off a wing, before the tree had cleared the hallway and he was exposed. Discovery imminent! He zoomed upstairs with as much as he could manage, a long piece of skin with fat and some flesh attached. He was content.

While he enjoyed his treat under Mrs. Clancy's bed, the evergreen tree stood in bare glory in a corner next to the range, with everybody admiring it before it should receive its decorations of streamers, wrapped nuts and bonbons, painted cones and bows, and the paper decorations they were to make tonight, gold and silver paper to be twirled and twisted into ribbons. Mr. and Mrs. Coll had never had a Christmas tree before, and had spent far more than they could afford to make this Christmas memorable for their little girl. It was worth it already—they could see the wonder in her eyes.

Then followed one of the happiest Christmas Eves ever in the Coll household, and it was because of the presence of a child. Bella sat on the hearthrug in front of the tree and glowed with happiness. Even Nana getting into bad humour about Tufty—when his absence and his crime was finally discovered—didn't spoil the night. The tree shone, twinkled, and sparkled before her; it seemed to wink at her, and when Mamma hung up the stockings, Bella thought herself completely happy. They sat around drinking hot chocolate and sang carols to welcome Baby Jesus. Like many a child on Christmas Eve, she tried hard to keep her eyelids open, but was defeated by fatigue and finally dropped off in her Papa's arms, her head snuggled against his flour-streaked shirt.

She had no nightmare that night.

CHAPTER SEVEN

On Christmas Morning, the wonder continued. Father Christmas had come, and been very generous to Bella. She had a big orange, wrapped sweets and nuts, new clothes for herself, and a new set of clothes for Maria to wear. The family went to church and sung carols there with gusto. Afterwards, a walk with Papa was suggested, to give the women room to prepare the Christmas Dinner. She held his hand tightly. The streets were quiet, only walkers like themselves and an occasional carriage or cart. Every business had shut up shop.

"Papa," she began. "My other Mama, my first Mama, came last night."

He tried not to react, but to take this as if it was the most natural thing in the world.

"Oh, and did she say anything?"

"She said I was to be happy, and she will see me again. I think my first Mama went to Heaven, Papa, and she's with Baby Jesus today. Maybe she has to help to look after Him in Heaven."

"That's very good indeed," Papa said, a little confused inside himself. "So you think your first Mama is in Heaven now?"

"Yes, she told me she was. Papa, look! That lady has such a funny hat, like a flowerpot turned upside down!"

"Hush! She might hear you, Bella!" He tipped his hat to the old woman with a cane, who was walking by, who indeed had a very odd hat.

He wouldn't go back to the other subject. The opportunity had passed, and he did not in any case wish to jog her memories about what had happened. Whatever it was, she was getting the better of it.

But he could hardly wait to tell Sophie. What a wonderful Christmas! They went home to the aroma of roast goose and pork and onion stuffing filling the house.

After serving dinner and washing the pots in the scullery, Molly departed the Colls with the goose carcass, and with more flesh attached than Mrs. Clancy would have liked, though Sophie claimed to have stripped it. Molly had the following day off, and her mother could make a good broth that would last her large family for a few days.

Sophie produced a custard trifle with cream, and she was happy to see it enjoyed by everybody. She and her mother cleaned off the table while Jim, Bella, and Tufty all cuddled up together on the sofa, sound asleep in the heat of the fire.

"Look at them, Mother! I'm so happy this day, I don't think anything could make me happier!" she said as she put the Willow-pattern platter in its place on the top shelf of the dresser. She did not yet know that Jim had something of importance to tell her, and when Bella was again asleep that night, and his mother-in-law gone up to bed, he drew her on his lap and related the conversation. She buried her head in his neck and wept for joy and gratitude.

"It doesn't matter if it was a dream or a real vision," she said. "The important thing is that she's peaceful."

CHAPTER EIGHT

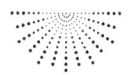

**E**very Boxing Day, the Colls made the journey from Whitechapel to Marylebone to visit their relations on Jim's side.

"I declare, they are on time," Lydia Hardwicke said in a tired voice. She had been peering out the fringed purple velvet curtains. "And they brought the waif."

"I hope they were not observed by anybody from Vickery, Norris & Burch. I have to inform Mr. Vickery, of course, of our unfortunate new connection, should we not be able to persuade your brother to give her up. For Mr. Vickery to discover it on his own, would be very detrimental to me."

Mrs. Hardwicke tossed her head.

"You don't have to tell him, Percy. Remember I have to deal with his horrid wife at our dinners."

"You call Mrs. Vickery horrid! Such a lady, her uncle a Baron. Sometimes, Lydia, your origins betray you."

*"Peace and Goodwill* lasts only one day of the year for you, Percy."

"Oh, shut up." was the reply.

"I suppose *I* will have to answer the door," Lydia said bitterly, as their three servants, two maids and a man, had Boxing Day off. But she greeted her relations as if they were the most dear to her in the world.

"So this is your new arrival," gushed Lydia. "Such a pretty girl, pert with it, I daresay."

Since Bella had not opened her mouth to speak, this was a wild foray into her character.

Jim looked at his sister in some surprise, while Mrs. Clancy set her lips in a tight line. She only accompanied them every year to make sure that Jim and Sophie did not agree to some harebrained scheme of Percy's that involved them having to invest money they did not have. It had happened a few years back, and nothing had come of it at all, only the loss to them of five pounds. They never saw the bad in anybody! She was sharper than both of them put together.

Lydia offered her cheek to her younger brother for a peck. Ten years old when he had been born, she'd been very jealous over the fuss made of the new baby. He had loved her without condition and always looked up to her, but she didn't have an affectionate nature and resented him. She had hated everything about her life in Whitechapel; uncouth neighbours, foreign sailors, unfashionable women, ragged children, costermongers, constant shouting of *Apples Cheap!* or *New Milk!* She had been born for better places than the East End. She had the good fortune to be very pretty, and she got work as a nanny in Marylebone, and attracted the attention of Percy Hardwicke when she was out walking her charges in the Park. He was an up-and-coming clerk in the offices of Vickery, Norris & Burch, Attorneys at Law. She'd set out to get him. She did not love him. He loved her—at first. But a few years after their second child was born, he began to stray. Perhaps some of that was her fault, she preferred to sleep alone and locked her door. That made him furious, but he consoled himself by going out at night and often stayed out until dawn. She stopped asking him where he had been, because he would snort and say: *"Where do you think I have been? At the*

*White Hart (or the Ten Bells), surely you know them well."* He had not been in the East End of course, he could find all the vice he wanted in places nearer to home. He was merely taunting her, because she hated the place where she grew up.

The husband and wife were agreed on one thing however, and that was by hook or by crook, they should get all the money they could lay their hands on. In this, they were a very good match.

"The children cannot wait to meet the new arrival!" she cried, as she ushered the party into the dining-room where they were to eat without delay. "Henry! Lucy!"

Two children appeared, many years older than Bella. They stared at her with curiousity. Mother and Father said she was a foundling, and that Uncle Jim should have taken her to the workhouse. She was very much below them, but Lucy had to admit she had pretty hair tied up in a red bow, and her red coat and plaid dress was almost as good as any she owned herself.

Dinner was rather miserable with the servants off. Mrs. Clancy was silently critical. Everything was served stone-cold. Could the hostess not have tossed the leftovers of the turkey into a frying-pan with some gravy, could she not have turned the mashed potatoes into a pot and heated them up? Without her servants, Mrs. Hardwicke was evidently helpless. The trifle had collapsed inwards, the custard running in little steams to the centre. The tea was hot though, and here Mrs. Hardwicke became ostentatious, the service was fine silver. The Christmas cake had had most of the icing removed, probably by the children.

"Take Bella away with you to play," instructed Lydia after the children had finished eating.

"And be nice! No fighting!" But Lydia was looking at Bella, not her own children as she got up to usher them towards the door. Bella looked up at her in astonishment. She had her doll tucked under her arm; Maria, resplendent in a new red and green tartan dress, with hat and jaunty feather to match, went everywhere with her. Bella looked as if she would rather not go, and looked behind at her mother, but Sophie encouraged her. She wished her to make friends with her cousins.

"So where did she come from?" asked Percy after the door shut.

"We told you all in a letter," Sophie said, astounded.

"Ah, yes, but where is she *from*? Do you know who her mother is? She could be anybody. I'm not throwing cold water on your choice to keep her, but you must be careful, for if she has not the—*breeding*—she may turn out just like her."

"Surely, Percy, you're not suggesting her mother was a woman of loose morals?" Jim said, amazed.

"She speaks—spoke—of Mama and Papa," Sophie said quite firmly. "That would strongly suggest to me that they were married. But even if her mother was the most immoral woman in all London, I would not care, not one bit. God loves her and so do we."

"I cannot argue with you there, but forgive me, sister, I was merely attempting to warn you, that it might not turn out well, I would hardly think myself a good brother to you and Jim if I did not," Percy continued.

"She's—dark. Is she fully English?" asked Lydia. "And a Christian?"

"She's English and a Christian now," said Jim in his usual calm manner. "As to where she was born, or who she was born to, that is not a matter that concerns us. She's a Coll."

In the parlour, Lucy and Henry had decided to play Blind Man's Buff, and Bella was to have the blindfold first. "See if you can find us!" chortled Lucy. "You have to put your two hands in front of you, like this, to find us, so you have to put your doll down."

Bella obeyed. They tied a scarf around her eyes, and all was dark. She did not like it, but wanted to please her new cousins.

"Find us! Find us!" cried Lucy and Henry together. Bella walked around the room, trying to find somebody with her hands, but all had gone quiet. She thought she heard the door click open and shut, and she heard excited laughter from the hallway. She followed the sounds into the hallway. But she had had enough of this silly game, and pulled the scarf off. She was just in time to see Maria flying helter-skelter though the air, her skirt over her head showing her white pantaloons. Henry was at one end of the hall, his sister at the other, throwing her to each other like a ball.

"Stop, stop!" she cried, raising her hands high and trying to catch Maria. But she knocked against a small table, and there was a crash as a vase there fell to the ground in smithereens.

In the resultant interrogation by the adults, Bella's cousins said that they were not throwing the doll at all, but only playing, making her part of the game. They said that it was Bella's fault that the vase broke, not theirs. They were nowhere near to the table. There was no doubt in the Hardwickes' minds that Bella was a troublemaker.

The family took their leave soon after. The Colls and Mrs. Clancy felt very upset, not that Bella had broken a vase, but that she had suffered at the hands of her older cousins, whose actions went beyond the normal teasing, and was spiteful, given that she was so much younger than they. They politely offered to pay for the vase, but Lydia shook her head. It was irreplaceable, she pronounced, leaving the Colls to wonder if it had come from distant parts, or whether it had been a Hardwicke heirloom. But Mrs. Clancy knew the type of vase well. There were fifty similar vases in every shop in town.

Lydia watched them out the gate with relief as they made their way to the train station.

"That girl will be trouble," she said to George. "Bad breeding. And now she will be spoiled. My brother is so dull! Did you see the way they believed her, that the breakage was an accident? She has them in her power. Now I have to sweep up the broken bits, since there is nobody else to do it. That vase was a perfect match for the wallpaper. Where does Annie keep the broom? Are you not even listening?" she shot at her husband.

"I'm not so concerned about the vase as I am about the future of Number 3 Lupin Lane." Was her husband's reply as he stoked the fire.

"What, you don't think the bakery and the house will ever be left to *her*," cried his wife. "That's Henry's. Not that he will ever live or occupy himself there, but as you have often said, the land it sits on will become valuable because of the railways."

"Of course, they will leave it to her. Can't you see that?"

"We have fixed on that being Henry's; we shall prevent it, Percy."

"By every means that we can." replied her husband.

CHAPTER NINE

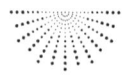

January's cold robbed London's East End of many inhabitants. By the time February came, the population was heartily sick of winter. Everybody had suffered colds, many several in a row. Some had become ill with fevers and chest infections. The widow Mrs. Foster died of pneumonia. Her children had to be sent to the Whitechapel Union Workhouse. Ned Smith, the lad from Number 2, succumbed to tuberculosis; his brother was consumptive also and would not see summer. The London Hospital overflowed with patients. People were afraid to go in there when they were ill, as they might catch something worse and die.

The Colls had their share of illness, but all recovered, and spring and summer passed, that last season bringing its share of warm weather illnesses, again disposing of Whitechapel's vulnerable population through cholera and intestinal diseases spread through bad water and poor sanitation. Philip and Gracie lost their baby brother, John, born only a few months before.

Whitechapel was becoming more crowded with emigrants; Irish who had been evicted from their cabins; Jews fleeing persecution elsewhere; and as always, the steady stream of poor country folks thinking they would have a better life in the City, only to find out that they were worse off than before.

Mrs. Smith now needed the Colls' charity, and received it, but unable to pay rent or to buy essentials, she had no choice after her second son died but to be admitted to the Union Workhouse, where she herself died shortly after. Number 2 Lupin Lane was sold, and became a doss-house, a convenient venue for those too drunk to walk home from The Foremast, or whoever wanted a cheap bed for the night.

"We should be pleased with the extra orders for bread." Sophie said to her mother. "But of all places to bring up a girl properly! It's only a step away from being a house of vice, Mother!"

They could, of course, move to other premises, but Jim would not hear any talk of it. He would rather move to Mars.

"You instill good morals into Bella as she grows, and she will not fall into any trouble," her mother replied with conviction. "You have to be a little stricter with her, Sophie. You noticed she is a little stubborn and has a little temper when provoked? Quell it, Sophie."

"Oh, I do, Mother, when she has calmed down, I have a little chat with her! Then she is always so sorry! So full of penitence! She will go to the moon and back for any of us!"

"That I know, my dear."

Philip began his apprenticeship that year, and very proud he was too, to pass from boyhood to manhood. He learned quickly, and soon grasped the Account Book, and for the next few years, became expert not just at baking Household Bread but also at the fluctuating prices of flour, sugar, and other goods, for he also read the financial part of the newspapers, and as he had a friendly, open nature, struck up conversations with accountants, buyers, and even customs officers, as to how it was that prices rose and fell. In time, he was even able to get tips of changes in the market, and he stocked up when prices were about to go up and held off when they were about to come down. In this way he was very valuable to Jim, who began to depend on his knowledge and judgement.

As Bella grew up, she learned all the skills of housekeeping as well as dressmaking and knitting. Her mother taught her how to read and write, Philip taught her arithmetic for a few extra bob. In 1880, school became compulsory, but by then she was about ten years old, and did not have to go. She spent a lot of her time in the bakery, and there learned skills also, but she wanted to experiment with pastry. She wanted Papa to expand into Confectionery, and he told her she could do it herself if she was willing to put the work in.

They celebrated her birthday on Mayday, not knowing exactly when her birthday was, but it was always a good day, before the heat of summer brought its troubles. London's air felt better then—many had left off coal fires, and the air was purer. They closed the bakery early and went on an outing by train, bringing sandwiches. Philip accompanied them. He felt as much part of this family as his own, and well before he was twenty-five, when Bella was eighteen, toyed with the idea of staying in it forever.

Molly got married, and her young sister Bridie took her place. Mrs. Clancy remained strong as ever, happy in her boarding house, and though people were dying all around her, as she put it, she was hale and hearty. She was devoted to Bella and Bella to her, though she no longer came to stay. She said that the little room was now Bella's, but the real reason was that she could not sleep a wink with the noise in the doss-house next door, for sometimes they had very loud music, pianos and raucous singing, and she was convinced that was to cover other more shameful shenanigans. Number 1 on the other side had fallen vacant some time ago, and the owner of Number 2, Mrs. Wilcox, had bought it up and made renovations to accommodate her entertainment shows, though it still bore the sign: *Lupin Lane Lodging House.* A few neighbours tried to get her evicted, but to no avail.

Jim became sick with what the doctor said was a weak heart, leaving more and more of the bakery affairs to Sophie and Philip, and in time, Bella, while he spent much time upstairs resting.

CHAPTER TEN

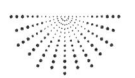

"I don't know why Uncle Percy and Aunt Lydia want me over to their house to stay," Bella grumbled, frowning at the letter in her hand. "One thing I'm sure of, Mamma, I'm not going."

Sophie took the flatiron from the range top and it made a *thump, thump* as she worked it to and fro on the cotton shirt spread on a blanket on the table.

"I think you should accept," she said, after a pause.

"Oh Mamma, you know I hate it there!"

Ever since Bella's first visit to Marylebone she had gone there with no pleasure. If she had only known it, Sophie felt the same.

"Can you write and say you cannot spare me?" Bella urged.

"I think you should go."

*Thump, thump* went the iron while Bella waited for the explanation.

"I think you should get to know them better, Bella. Lucy is grown and married; Henry will be busy, he's gone into the same firm as his father. It's not good to be rowing with your relatives. When they know you better, they will love you. Go and allow them to get to know you."

Bella sighed. She went into the bakery where Philip was busy serving customers. It was Mrs. Wilcox, the landlady next door.

"I'll have a dozen of those lemon tartlets," she said.

Bella smiled. She it was who had made the lemon tartlets, and all of the pastry items that they carried. She loved baking pastry, had a light hand, and fruit tartlets were her specialty. But many people could not afford them, so every morning, she took some fresh sweet buns and the tartlets and put them on a large tray which she hung around her neck and sold them on High Street cheaper than if they sold them from the bakery. They went quickly.

"Ah Miss Coll," said Mrs. Wilcox. "Was it you I heard singing last night? You have a beautiful voice."

Bella blushed. She loved singing. She sang for her father when he asked her to, songs that Bridie had taught her. Bridie knew a lot of songs. But it embarrassed her to be heard by anybody. She wondered who else could hear her sing! Some of the men who frequented Mrs. Wilcox's establishment?

"I have entertainments," she went on. "I'm always looking for new talent, like yours. Would you care to come along next Saturday evening and sing for me? I'll pay you."

"Oh, thank you, but no." Bella said quickly, thinking of what her father and mother would say to that.

"Some other evening, then. You could have a very good career, singing. Well, good day, then." Mrs Wilcox left.

"I was afraid you'd say yes," Philip remarked, grinning.

"What, how could I? My mother and Nana would kill me! Anyway, I'll be in Marylebone next Saturday night." She told Philip what was afoot.

Philip didn't like it. He had met the Hardwickes a few times, and did not like Henry. A few years ago, he had come to visit, ostensibly to see his ailing Uncle. A Jack the Lad, and a dandy, was Mr. Henry

Hardwicke. He'd swaggered about the back, kicked the bags of flour for no apparent reason, pulled open sugar bags, called the furnaces ancient, and then said that it would be his one day.

"But don't think I'll occupy myself baking bread," he'd said, sniggering. "I'll sell this place to the Metropolitan Railway. They're expanding all the time. When Uncle snuffs it, not that I want that to happen." He added hastily.

"What if the Metropolitan don't want it?"

Henry hadn't appeared to have thought of that.

"I'll buy up the neighbours' houses, pull them all down, and build houses with rooms to let. Like that place you live in."

"Has Mr. Coll told you he'll leave you the bakery?" Philip felt bold enough to ask.

"That's none of your business. You don't know your place, do you?"

Philip went on doing his Accounts. Henry came behind him and peered over his shoulder. Philip slammed the book shut.

"What are you hiding, Mitchell? Are you cheating my uncle?"

"No, but I don't work with someone breathin' down me neck."

"You have a nerve. When I get this place, you'll be gone."

"I could be gone anytime I like. I'm a Master Baker these three years."

"Why are you still here then? There are better bakeries, more modern than this hole in the wall."

"None of your business what I do, Mister."

Henry had come out from behind the counter and sauntered up and down the shop for a few minutes, before he turned and said:

"I have it, by Jove. You hang on here in hopes of—"

"Of what?" snapped Philip.

"I think you know what I mean. Well, she isn't going to get it. She isn't our blood. And if she's named as heir, I and my father will take her to court. We work for Vickery, Norris & Burch in the City."

"Never 'eard of 'em." Philip tossed his copper head in derision.

"You're backing a loser, Mitchell. A dead horse."

"I don' like the way you express yourself, Hardwicke." Philip's eyes hardened.

"*Mr.* Hardwicke to you."

Philip's knuckles began to itch. He could flatten this foppish idiot in half a second. He prayed for self-restraint. Bella came in just then from the street door. She had been selling on High Street.

"Good afternoon, Cousin Bella." Henry bowed and smiled insolently.

"Good afternoon." She made as if to pass him, but he blocked her way. Bella shrank a little. Though the incident when she was four years old had largely passed from her memory, she knew that she did not like Henry Hardwicke. He was nasty, a bully, and a tease.

Philip came to her rescue, as she felt a freezing come over her. Almost as if she were paralysed with fright. She did not know why this was! Why could she not stand up to this bully? He was smiling at her, almost leering.

"Excuse us, Hardwicke," Philip had said smoothly as he'd taken her arm and led her past him. With Philip beside her, she had recovered herself and walked easily.

Hardwicke's expression had changed from one of insolence to embarrassment.

"I will see you are out on the street soon," he had hissed to Philip.

"Do your worst," Philip had said mildly, opening the accounts again. Mr. Henry Hardwicke had not bothered him after that.

"What are you thinking of?" Bella chided him, bringing him back to the present. "I've been saying that both Mamma and Papa, him especially, feels that my aunt is making a friendly overture, and that it would be very rude not to go. So I must!"

Bella had grown into a beautiful young woman. Her dark hair she put up now; he rarely glimpsed it flowing as it used. Her eyes were clear, her skin with its olive tone, had not a blemish. Even grubby, sooty London seemed to bypass her while the dirt settled on others. Or so it seemed to Philip. He loved her, and he could detect no fault, except that occasionally, as that afternoon a few years ago, she could not stand up for herself. She needed a bit of bottle. He felt very protective toward her. He was afraid for her in the Hardwickes' home. They were not good people and this pretext of getting to know her better was a hoax. What did they really want? It had occurred to him that if Henry married Bella, then he would have all he wanted. Was that the intention, to get the young people acquainted with each other?

He wondered how Bella felt about him, Philip Mitchell? Did she have any special feeling, or was he simply a fixture of Coll's Bakery, like a piece of furniture? He hadn't much to offer, having come from Jerome's Buildings. He was a hard worker though, and intended to join the newly established *National Association of Master Bakers and Confectioners* as soon as he could afford the subscription of ten shillings and sixpence. He was mates with another Master Baker, John Quill, and together they had attended a meeting in Holborn last winter, which was open to non-members, and which he had found very educational.

"Be careful." he told her. "I'm sorry to say this of your relatives, but I don't fully trust 'em. Don't be alone with Mr. Henry there, unless you want to be," he added hastily.

"I don't want to be!" Bella's eyes flashed. "I haven't forgotten that time he came in here—and you came to my assistance—I don't know why I was frozen in fright that time. I'll make sure I'm never alone with him."

"Just remember then, Miss Bella, that bullies are always cowards, deep down. Think of him that way. It might help."

"You're a true friend, Philip." She smiled, and his heart leaped, but she had said 'friend.' All the same, it was a start.

CHAPTER ELEVEN

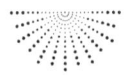

Bella was welcomed at 17 Pollock Street, Marylebone, with gracious kindness. She was shown to her room. Thankfully, there was no sign of the heinous Henry. Her room was very nice, much larger than any she had slept in. The window looked out on a garden.

She went down to dinner, wearing her best dress. Thankfully, no Henry at dinner either! She would not even ask where he was. Her hosts made good general conversation without really saying anything much. She had brought letters and they appeared to be appreciated.

The following day they took her out to Vauxhall Gardens. She repented her reluctance to come and visit them; they were showing her every attention, were even very solicitous of her. Everybody deserved a second chance, she thought, knowing her ill father would be very happy to know how good they were being to her. She looked forward to telling him all after she returned home. The next day was just as pleasant, Aunt Lydia took her to Chelsea on the train, where they walked about and visited the shops.

But on her last evening, after dinner, they said they wished to have a serious conversation with her, and she felt that all was not as well as she thought.

"We are fearful of your father and mother's future," Lydia began, looking at her anxiously.

"Papa is not in good health, it is true, but the doctor says he is not to exhaust himself with long hours in the business, and if he rests enough, he will recover."

The couple looked at each other. Anxiety stabbed Bella's heart.

"What is it?"

"We are afraid that this news will affect him in a very adverse manner," Lydia said. "for it is not good news."

"What are you talking about? What can be wrong?"

Her Uncle got up from his chair and went to the window.

"Tell her, Lydia, it is more proper coming from you."

Her aunt turned her face toward her. Bella could not but feel that her eyes had a rather superior, hard look.

"It concerns a letter, Bella. A very unexpected letter from a very unexpected source. About you."

"Me?"

"Or rather, about your *origins.*"

"Oh." Bella frowned. She had dim, very dim memories of the time before she came to Lupin Lane. What had the Hardwickes heard?

"This will come as a great shock to you, Bella, and I do feel for you, I honestly feel for you, as if you were our own flesh and blood."

Bella did not like the reminder that she was not their own flesh and blood.

"We—or rather—the firm Mr. Hardwicke works for, Vickery, Norris & Burch, have received a letter from a woman who says she is your natural mother."

"My mother!"

"Yes. Here is the letter."

Bella took it into her trembling hands.

*Gentlemen*

*I trust you will do me the honour of attending to my business, that is, of putting me in contact with my daughter Isabella, who now must be about eighteen years old. I have found out, by very circuitous means that she is with a family, near relations of the Hardwicke family members of whom I know work in your offices. I wish to see my girl, and would you be so good as to arrange this. I have the resources to remunerate you in any and all expenses you charge for this service. I wish to see my daughter again before I die. Yours truly, Blanche duBarry.*

Bella looked at this and exhaled a long breath she had been holding. She sat back in her armchair, astonished beyond belief, her heart beating rapidly.

"I know it's been a shock," Aunt Lydia said. "But, there is more." She glanced over at her husband by the window, but he merely nodded at her.

"We have felt it incumbent to make inquiries about this woman, Blanche duBarry. Bella, dear, you must prepare yourself for an even greater shock."

"What is it?" Bella's olive tones had turned white.

"She is a woman of ill-repute. She is notorious in a certain district of our City, for her parties and—houses she runs, where men go to obtain the favours of women, bad women, Bella. That class of fallen, immoral, and sinful women who betray those of us who are respectable!" Lydia's voice had become raised and angry, and she stared at her husband's back as he looked out the window, instead of looking at her, which Bella found odd.

"Mr. Harwicke?" she rapped.

He walked abruptly back to her. His wife rose from her chair. They both loomed before her.

"If this gets to my dear brother, it will ruin him! It may kill him!" Lydia was becoming hysterical.

"I don't agree—" Bella began, but Uncle Percy had thundered his contribution right after his wife's and did not hear her.

"There is only one thing to be done, if you have any regard for your parents, and for all of your benefactors. You must leave London. Immediately. Do not visit this disgrace upon them or upon our family, the Hardwickes. It is unconscionable that we should be associated with this brothel-owner, a Jezebel, a Babylonian—"

"Stop, do not say that word in my presence!" Aunt Lydia shouted angrily at him.

"Please listen to me—" Bella pleaded, but they did not even hear her plea to be listened to, so there was no hope of their listening to what she was about to say.

"There is only one thing to be done in all this," Mr. Hardwicke said. "You must leave London tomorrow. We are prepared to give you five pounds to travel North, and never come back. You may get yourself a position as a domestic servant, or a seamstress, do whatever you wish. But never come back here."

Bella rose up. She felt herself freeze again, but remembered Philip's good, wise face encouraging her. But it was not Henry she had to fight! It was her Uncle and Aunt!

"Please listen to me. This is not true." She felt herself tremble in terror, but stand up to them she must.

"True? Of course it is true. We have made independent inquiries, and—"

"And what?" Bella asked. "What have your enquiries uncovered? How did I come to be at Lupin Lane?"

They seemed stumped. As if they had not expected this rally.

"You are the child of a drunken foreign sailor," said Lydia, with disgust. "The result of an hour of debauchery and grossness, such as low foreigners are apt to indulge in when in ports-of-call."

"Is that what your enquiries have uncovered?" Bella said with impudence, and more bravery than she felt. She trembled but she held her ground.

They did not answer her.

"Tomorrow morning, we will call a Hansom cab for you to take you to the Railway and you will leave this house, and this city," her uncle said. "Take your five pounds now." He threw a small packet at her feet. "You will leave no note for your parents, and you will not contact them in any way."

"This cannot be true," Bella said, her voice shaking, but slow and firm. "You allege that this woman, who claims to be my mother, wants to see me. But, I have known, for a very long time, that my natural mother, as you call her, is dead."

They seemed very taken aback, and Lydia fell back into her chair.

"You cannot possibly know that, Bella. How did you come to be outside the window of my brother's bakery? Who brought you there?"

Bella trembled again, for the memories threatened to rise from their graves and engulf her in terror. But she held her feet firmly on the carpet, and said:

"I don't remember. But I know my mother is dead and that you've been vastly taken in, or else have been victims of a cruel hoax." She walked away, and shut the door after her, the packet of money still on the carpet.

"I will leave tomorrow," she said, through the door. "But not for the North. I'm going home—home to Lupin Lane!"

She lay in bed, shivering, wishing she could get up and go home now. Memories flashed by like spirits appearing and vanishing before she could catch them. She had always had a memory of a beautiful, dark-haired woman. She knew it was her mother. She remembered her flowing dressing gown, light-blue, soft and silky to touch, and how she used to sing her to sleep in her little cot. She must have got her voice from her mother.

Later, they had been on a ship. And something horrible had happened after they got into a port. She couldn't remember anymore, except for that first Christmas she had in Lupin Lane, when she had a Christmas tree. Just before she had fallen asleep with the Christmas tree in her view, trying her best not to close her eyes, she had seen her first mother beside it, smiling and telling her she was in Heaven and that she was to love her new Mama and Papa, and that's how she knew. She remembered telling her father that, when they were out for a walk, just before they had seen the woman with the funny hat. She wondered now what he had made of it. She wondered now if she had dreamed it all, but it had seemed so real!

She left the following morning before breakfast, walking out of the house before anybody was up.

Her aunt and uncle were furious at the outcome.

"I'm not giving up," said Mr. Hardwicke at breakfast, after dismissing the maid from the room. "That bakery is Henry's by rights. She's not going to inherit it. And I don't see why our good name should be dragged through the courts either, even though we would win, if there's any justice in England. That letter you wrote was not effective, Lydia."

"And how would I know how a—woman like that—would write a letter?" she retorted. "You should 'ave gotten one of your lady friends to write it."

*"Have,* not *'ave."* He corrected her. "When you are agitated, my dear, you slip back to your origins."

"I will drag your name through the courts one day, Mr. Hardwicke. And these women I'll produce for the Judge, will be real women, not inventions like Blanche duBarry!"

"You would not dare!" he cried. "You would ruin us all, for revenge?"

"I think about it more and more," she said. "But if Bella Coll disappears forever, never to return, I might not proceed."

"Disappear forever! You cannot mean—you cannot be asking me to—"

"I will give you the rest of the year to think about it. If she is still with us in 1889, I will divorce you, and ruin you. I will go and live with Lucy. And—I have the names of your—" again, she could not say the word, but rose from the table, and left the room.

CHAPTER TWELVE

"I am back safely, as you see!" Bella said to Philip. "No Henry at all, thank God! But that doesn't mean there wasn't trouble!" She told him all. Philip was so easy to confide in. He understood everything. He was shocked.

"I don't know who sent that letter to them," Bella said. "But they were really taken in. It wasn't nice of them to try and make me vanish, was it?"

Philip had his own opinion as to the origin of the letter and the person named 'Blanche duBarry' but he was not about to say.

"If you had done a bunk, that would've been the worst thing for your parents."

"Oh, I knew that. They can't understand that my parents love me, and would be heartbroken if I was to leave suddenly and they never to hear from me forevermore."

"You're very much loved, Bella." Philip said, blushing deeply as he said so, and half-turning away. Bella, however, did not seem to notice. She had gone on to say how she knew that this woman, if she existed, could not be her mother. She told Philip about her memories of the dark-haired woman with the silk dressing gown, who used to sing her to sleep.

*She's gentry*, thought Philip in some dismay. *Way above me an' all. Gentry. And she doesn't even seem to know it herself.*

He did not want Bella to find out anymore about herself, but that was selfish. However, she did not seem to be very curious anyway.

Jim Coll began to feel much better; as the year went on, he was coming downstairs to work again. He had utter confidence in his assistant, but his new ideas perturbed him somewhat, so Philip felt it wiser to keep them to himself, after Mr. Coll had wondered, in astonishment, why in the world modern bakers were pursuing scientific tests, the better to make bread. In his opinion, if a man knew his craft well, he didn't need to rely on experiments. He had it all in his head, no, in his little finger. Bella was present at this conversation and she was amused.

"Don't be disappointed," she said to Philip later as she lingered in the bakery to talk, as was her habit. "He's just a bit old-fashioned."

"I'm not disappointed," Philip replied. "It's just that the science of how it all works together, yeast and barm and flour and what-have-you, and new technologies in baking methods are interesting. But I'll keep my ideas under my hat."

Bella wondered why Philip did not strike out on his own. She supposed it cost a lot of money to begin a business. He was probably saving. But that would be difficult, given that his father had died and he was supporting his mother and youngest sister. The other two were in service. She and Gracie rarely saw each other now.

The summer came and her 18th birthday in May was celebrated with happiness. Her father was better, and that was the best gift of all.

"Why doesn't Philip speak?" Mrs. Clancy asked Sophie, seeing the young people set off together to the top of Primrose Hill, to take in the fine views of the City. The two women were sitting on a bench, the picnic basket open beside them. Jim was pacing about. Primrose Hill was all very well, but as usual, it gave him a very odd feeling to be in a strange place such as this.

"Philip is a bit shy, I suppose. Or, perhaps it's money. Yes, I suppose that's it."

"Would you like him for Bella?"

"Yes, Mother, and I would very much like him for me, for a son-in-law!"

"He has no money at all, Sophie. I don't object to him at all, though," she added with haste. "He's a good, solid lad. Does she like him, do you think?"

"It's hard to know what she feels sometimes. I don't like to ask her, in case she doesn't want to tell me yet."

"How long will they be?" asked Jim, coming by.

"Oh, Jim! Let the young people have time to themselves. Sit down and have another sandwich. Do you want ox-tongue or jam? I enjoy the change of scenery as well, I do!"

CHAPTER THIRTEEN

"Another murder, another poor unfortunate." Philip said one morning, after he had come in from a delivery around George's Yard. He had come into the living-room for a moment, had been asked, as always, if there was any news in the neighbourhood. He had no other details, and disappeared again for the bakery.

"Why are there so many women murdered?" asked Bella. "Why are they out alone, so late at night?" she knew the answer, but wanted to talk to her mother about it.

"They're prostitutes." said Sophie quietly. "Poor women. Remember when we took bone broth down to the Kellys in Petticoat Lane? Remember how poor the families were? The wet floors, the smells, the rat droppings? Some of the women sell themselves for food; others drink too much. They can meet drunken, violent men in their work. The worst kind!"

"The building Philip lives in is almost as crowded and poor as Petticoat Lane. That's why he sleeps here on sacks in the bakery, isn't it? And Mama—is Mrs. Wilcox's a place where men go—for—women?" Bella asked. This question had been burning her for a long time, but she had been afraid to ask.

"We hope not, but we don't know what goes on in there." Sophie said.

"She's invited me in a few times, to sing."

"Don't darken that doorstep, Bella!" her mother seldom flared in anger or any strong emotion, and Bella smiled. She had no intention of 'darkening the doorstep' of the premises next door.

"Don't worry, Mamma." she laughed.

"Some people act as if there's no Judgement Day," said Mrs. Clancy darkly to nobody in particular. Getting a little infirm, she often stayed with them now and was even thinking of moving in. Bella had no objection to sharing her room with her grandmother, and Mrs. Clancy had learned to close her ears to the shenanigans from next door.

"Such noise tonight!" murmured Bella, waking up an hour or so after she had gone to sleep one night late in September. She slept on a thin mattress on the floor, allowing her grandmother to have the small bed to herself. She heard shouts, running feet, and police whistles. She drifted back to sleep.

She arose early to bake her pastries. She enjoyed arranging them on the tray and going out and selling them in High Street. It was a busy, brisk place, with shops and street sellers, all of whom she knew. It was filled with costermongers, men and women selling everything one could need—candles, scrap metal, flowers, fruit, even hot food. She had a word for everybody, and they for her.

"I don't think you should go out today," Philip said when she appeared, two cups of tea in her hand. She always brought him a cup of tea and a few biscuits. "There was two murders last night. There's a lot of coppers about. Whitechapel and Spitalfields is swarmin' with them. Did you not hear the whistles, then?"

"I did, they woke me. Murders, of women, you mean? *Unfortunates?*"

"Yes. Jack the Ripper."

"Why do they call him that? It's horrible!"

"The murders are particularly horrible. Too bad to talk of. Stay in, will you, Bella? Your father would be upset if you went out."

"Don't tell him then!" Bella rejoined, uncovering the pastry which had been resting all night and taking up the rolling-pin. She went about her work on the floured table, humming. "Will you bake a few extra dozen sweet buns, Philip—those coppers might be hungry," she said. "Might as well feed 'em."

"You ain't half an opportunist, Bella!" said Philip good-humouredly.

"Oh, do you think that's awful?" Bella said, her mouth opening in an O.

"No harm in it. Coppers will be hungry, as you say. It's our duty to look after our men in blue as well as the populace of Whitechapel and Spitalfields."

"As long as I don't feed the murderer unbeknownst. Philip, how would I know if someone was a murderer?"

"I told you—advised you—not to go out. Tell you what, I'll go out instead of you, today."

"No, you won't, Philip. I'm going!"

She said the same thing to her father when he appeared around eight o'clock. He hadn't the interest in quarrelling with her and merely waved his hand and said: "You go with her, Philip. I'll be here for the morning anyway. Don't look so smug, girl, you 'ave a stubborn streak, Missy. Go back and have your cuppa, both of you, and then be off."

"Oh thank you, Papa!" she kissed his cheek. They went to the living-room for their breakfast. Mrs. Coll had heard the whistles as well and was none too pleased that her father had given her permission to go out, but was relieved that Philip was going, too.

As soon as Bella had taken two dozen still-warm rolls from the rack, they set off, walking on the cobbles under the archway into Lupin Street, and soon reached the hullabaloo and din of High Street.

"Black with coppers!" she exclaimed, as they walked along, past the shops that were just opening, Massey's Grocers among them.

"You don't stand there outside my shop," Mr. Massey said to her. She and Mr. Massy had a running battle over territory.

"I thought I'd bring you more custom," she replied brightly. "When people stop, they can see your signs, what you have off today, and the like."

"You block my signs," he replied testily.

"He started selling baked goods, you see," Bella explained to Philip. "Mornin' Constable, care for a sweet bun?"

The constable looked about to make sure his sergeant wasn't anywhere in the vicinity, paid her two pennies and took one.

"How's the murder investigation going?" Philip asked.

"Sorry, mister, can't tell you nothing; it's all confidential," he said. He bit into the bun.

"Where were you last night?" he asked Philip, probably to justify his stopping on his beat.

"I was at work, sir. Master Baker at Coll's Bakery, 3 Lupin Lane."

"Hear anything out of the ordinary?"

"Only a lot of shoutin' and whistles, Constable."

"Hope you get the monster!" cried out a man on a passing milk cart. "Terrorisin' good people, 'e is! The rope will be too good for the loikes of 'im!"

This was met with a chorus of assent from several other street sellers and passers-by.

"What's Gracie doing back in Whitechapel?" asked Bella suddenly.

"Where's Gracie?" Philip wheeled around to where her eyes had wandered.

"Isn't she supposed to be in Highgate? Maybe she left her situation. Gracie!" called Bella, to the slight, fair-haired figure she had spotted in the throngs of people. But Gracie either did not hear, or she chose not to, as she disappeared from view.

"That's a bit odd, that," she murmured to herself. "Maybe she just got the day off."

"Ma said she hadn't heard from her for a bit," Philip said, wonderingly.

"Go after her, Philip!"

"I have to stay with you, don't I? Anyway, I don't know where she's got to."

"Sweet bun, Constable, fresh, baked only this morning!" Bella was not allowing any custom to get away, as another bobby passed by.

"I say, Constable, will you tell this person to step away from my door, she's interfering with my trade!" Mr. Massey had come storming out.

"I have more important things on my mind!" snapped the policeman, walking away, while Mr. Massey grunted in anger and went back into his shop.

CHAPTER FOURTEEN

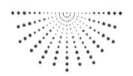

Grace Mitchell resolved never to leave the East End again. The devil you know is better than the devil you don't know, she thought to herself. She knew all about devils. Devils outside, devils inside. What was a girl to do with devils inside herself?

She'd first become acquainted with this devil one day when she was eleven years old, and Mr. Coote from upstairs had encountered her on the landing. There'd been nobody else there and he had overpowered her. She was left crumpled on the ground, shaking and sobbing, but didn't dare tell anybody, not her mother, who was harried from work and looking after their father, nor her father of course, who was ailing in bed. Not Philip, because she was ashamed. She kept her secret. Why had Mr.

Coote picked on her? Did she look like a bad girl? He made her feel that way, and over time she became sure that she was bad.

When she was fourteen, she'd gone into service in Highgate as a kitchen maid. It was a nice house, a lovely mistress, the housekeeper good, all in all a very good situation, and she had been happy there for two years, and thought she could stay there and work her way up to be Cook someday. Mr. Coote was just a horrid memory she put in her past. But one night, she had been working late in the kitchen, and a toff visitor to the House—her employer's nephew—came down and wanted the same thing Mr Coote had wanted. He didn't want to take no for an answer. But Gracie was older now and no longer a small girl, and she was wiry. Hard work had made her strong, and she slapped and even kicked him and he went away.

Instead of triumphing over her victory, she had instead sat down and wept. Was there something corrupted in her, that men thought they could take advantage? Did men see something evil in her, something even she could not see? She felt very despairing. Where was God? Did God condemn her because of this—evil demon hounding her? She could not stay in that house, of course, afraid to face that man the next day, so she packed her box and left that very night without giving notice.

In her second place, she had not discovered the freedom and peace she thought she would find, though it was an all-female household. With no references, she'd used a copy of the character reference she'd got from her parson, and very carefully changed the year to update it.

But she had felt weak and shattered, and found it so hard to get up and face the work of the day. She felt she never wanted to get up again, maybe for the rest of her days. Some days, she felt as if death would be preferable to the devils inside her, her thoughts, above all those of the horrible Mr. Coote who had taken her innocence and given her the demon in her thoughts. She could not stop thinking about what he had done.

One day, she'd noticed that the drinks cupboard in the dining-room was never locked. Just a sip, maybe, of something to help her nerves. She'd taken some sherry. After that, she sipped from all the different bottles in turn, then fearing discovery more than anything, she started to buy gin. But there was little privacy. She shared a room and had to drink it when Becky, the housemaid, could not see. And always there was the fear of discovery. She supposed that she knew she would be discovered someday—the housekeeper had found the bottle under her pillow, where she drank from it every morning before she got out of bed.

She had been dismissed from her second place without any reference.

It was all sordid and horrible, and she sank lower and lower in her own estimation. She really was good for nothing. Except *that*.

She felt doomed to perpetual misery and returned to Spitalfields, but not home to Whitechapel. Not yet. She had to get herself together, and try to convince herself to begin again, and to forget the past, if she could. She tried to pray, but was sure God was very angry with her and had been since she was eleven years old, or else why would He have let that happen to her?

She'd go and see her mother soon, but she had to think up a story. She knew she would be seen sometime, by one of the many people she knew; what would she tell them? Her only confidante was the colourless liquid that warmed her throat and somehow, by its properties, dulled her pain. But only for a little while, and then she needed more.

Gin was easy to get, as long as she had the money. But how to get money? She had no job, nor would she ever get a good situation again. She was only eighteen years old and she wished her life was over. She felt that she was only good for one employment, and that was to do what men wanted. She had failed at everything else.

She'd returned one week ago, and with her wages paid to her in lieu of notice, had put herself up for a week in a cheap boarding house. It was a horrible place, everything was dirty, but she felt she deserved no better.

On her first night in the house, she'd bumped into another woman on the landing, somewhat older than herself, but for all her cragged, used look, she had a motherly air and began to chat to her. Where was she from? How had she come to be in the boarding house? Alice had invited her out to The Ten Bells public house and, though she had her misgivings, she had gone. She had known full well what would transpire. Two sailors just off a ship soon struck up a conversation with them. Alice had gone with one, and Grace with the other.

As she'd sat on her bed after the sailor left, she wept bitterly and reflected that she was in this now for good. There was no escape.

The following night, the clients were a little slow coming to them in The Ten Bells, so she and Alice chatted a bit more.

"I think I know how you got into this," Alice said.

"How could you know?"

"Many of us started that way. Taken advantage of, when we were young. It takes somethin' away from you. It's not a good life, just so you know before you get in too deep. If I had a daughter I'd as likely kill 'er as let her live the life we do 'ere."

"That man who just came in, he's staring at me." Gracie said.

"That's Mooney. He's going to sweeten you up. He goes after all the the new girls, he'll tell you he's in love with you. Don't believe a word of it. Gracie. Don't fall in love wiv a man who buys you things and is nice to you, cos some girls go live wiv a man they fink is good, and find 'e just wants 'er to work for 'im. She 'as to bring 'im in money or else. More than one of us 'ave ended up in 'ospital from cuts and bruises and broken bones, even dead, from tryin' ter get away from men like that. I was lucky. My man kicked the bucket."

Alice then leaned over and whispered something in her ear.

"I will never do tha'! That's killin', that is!"

"You can't work if you're lyin'-in. If you can't work, he don't need you no more. You're out on your ear, you an' your child. The workus is where he'll grow up."

Gracie cupped her glass. A rising tide of despair welled in her heart. Dreams that she might have had when she was young, of falling in love, getting married to a good man who had his health and his trade, and having children and living in a house, maybe even like the Colls lived in, were faded. Bella! What would Bella think of her now? She wouldn't even speak to her anymore! Philip was sweet on Bella, and they would get married and be respectable, and she—she could not see any future for herself.

Alice elbowed her.

"Cheer up, Grace! We'll never get customers the way you is lookin' tonight! Be 'appy! C'mon over 'ere, Jonny is startin' the piano, let's 'ave a song. There's a ship comin' in later."

CHAPTER FIFTEEN

Mrs. Clancy's health began to decline. She spent more time in bed, and felt increasingly short of breath as the leaves blew that Autumn.

November 1888 came to Whitechapel. A typical November, wet, cold, muddy, sloshy, dirty, smoggy, grim, and dark. Many babies and old people in Jerome's Buildings succumbed to chest infections, and Mr. Pratt the Undertaker did a brisk business.

Bella had her Nana's health on her mind, but she also noticed that Philip had something on his. He seemed distracted, troubled, and one morning after he completely forgot to add sugar to the dough for the sweet buns, she asked him what was the matter.

"You won't like to hear it, Bella." He flushed and looked upset.

"Go on, Pip, are we not friends? Don't I tell you my troubles, then? You know them well! Is your mother well? Have you heard from Gracie yet?"

He looked even more miserable as he arranged the unsweetened buns on the rack.

"Don't worry about the buns—I'll make icing for the top—we got more icing sugar yesterday and I'll mix it with a bit of butter, and spread it over the tops. Now are you going to tell me?"

"It's Gracie," his voice was low and dejected. "You did see her that day—she's back. But not at home."

"Is she all right, Philip?"

He shook his head. "Not at all. You might as well hear the truth, as you will hear it anyway, from somebody or other. She's livin' in a house in Spitalfields. Dorset Street, I heard. It's been called the worst street in London. Where she's livin' is a house of ill repute, know what I mean, Bella?"

"Oh, Philip!" Tears filled Bella's eyes. She laid her hand on his arm.

"I suppose you won't want to know the Mitchells anymore," he said in a flat tone. "Your father and mother won't like to hear of this."

"Philip … what nonsense that is, Philip. Gracie is my childhood friend. All her troubles are mine, too. We can keep it to ourselves, just you and me. Perhaps she's just innocently boarding there …" her voice trailed off at the unlikelihood of this. "What misfortune happened to her? How did you find out? Does your mother know?"

He rubbed his face hard with both his hands, leaving them there, fingers crab-like, as if to stop tears. Bella waited patiently.

"She's a good girl." He said at last, his voice muffled.

"I know she is."

He took his hands from his face and began to rearrange the buns on the rack.

"She never gave the slightest bit of trouble, always kind, always good, hardworking at home, the apple of Father's eye. She was a good child, sweet, uncomplaining—"

"She's not dead, Pip." Bella interrupted him gently, a little amused even.

"Oh, Bella!" he said, "I don't know what to do. How can I go down to that place—and get her out of it? My greatest fear is that Ma will hear of it. She will find out sooner than later. Ma's had a hard life. Why this now? I was just about to get Ma into a better place, two rooms in Benner's Place, on the ground floor, with a little yard for a clothesline. But this might kill her. She always said that whatever else we din't have in life, we had our standards. She was so happy with that place in Highgate for Gracie. She said she'd be able to make something of herself there."

"How did you hear?"

"Some fellows shouted it after me in the street. I couldn't believe it. I went down there—to Dorset Street—and watched the place. I saw her and another woman come out of a house, Number 24—and I followed them to the Ten Bells Public House. That place has a bad name."

Bella's tears rolled down her cheeks. Gracie a 'fallen woman'!

"Something must've happened to her," she said, trying to recover herself and be strong for Philip. She thought of the women she saw coming and going from Wilcox's next door. How many of them had been good, kind women like Gracie, and fallen on some misfortune? But what had been Gracie's misfortune?

She resolved then to go to the boarding house on Dorset Street and see Gracie for herself. She could not tell anybody where she was going; it would have to be a secret. Her mother and father would be in an uproar.

CHAPTER SIXTEEN

Mr. Percy Hardwicke had mulled this matter over for long enough. The year would end soon, and he had to act. He did not know how his brother-in-law's health stood, but if he died this winter, he'd have to go to Court for the bakery. The other matter was more pressing. His wife had names of the women he had been unfaithful with; and they were all women who would make him a subject of public disgrace and derision everywhere he was known and respected. Lydia had not a care left about her own good name. She'd be happy to disgrace him and make herself look like a long-suffering victim. The wronged wife!

But he had to solve the *Bakery Question*, as he liked to call it to himself when he was mulling it over. He'd written down some possibilities in his study, where he spent hours mulling, and used up several sheets of notepaper with his thoughts.

1. Hire somebody.
2. Do not hire somebody, as that person, if caught, could name him
3. How to do it so as to leave no trace.
4. Shooting? Stabbing? Drowning?

The last appealed to him the most. Drowning could be made to look like an accident. He began to make further lists. How to get Bella into the River Thames? Luring her on some pretext, or kidnapping perhaps? This was quite a question. He wondered then if she would consent to taking an innocent walk with him. What if he and Lydia took her for a drive in a Hansom cab to the Tower Bridge, or some such, some out-of-the-way quayside? No, the cab driver would turn him in. He enjoyed the prospect of Lydia going to her fate, and even imagined it for a few moments with a smile, but then it came to the same fate for himself, and that he could not enjoy, so he dismissed the entire scenario.

He would have to involve somebody else if he hadn't the courage to do it himself, but ten pounds should be bribe enough for anybody to be involved in a murder.

CHAPTER SEVENTEEN

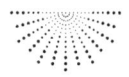

Bella planned to go and see Gracie as soon as she could. But she faced a dilemma—how could she leave her home unseen, without her parents knowing where she was going? But it had been a few months now since the last murders, and Whitechapel and Spitalfields had settled to normal life again. She would have to go in the morning with her tray of buns as usual, to High Street and having sold them, walk briskly to Dorset Street about 30 minutes away and find the doss house. She would have to explain her delay after she arrived home again. At eighteen years old, her parents were still very protective of her, she thought. But it was because of how she arrived at their door, that November afternoon all those years ago, and her heart melted when she thought of her dim memories of standing outside the window, and her Mamma and Papa coming out to take her into their home and their hearts. She did not remember anything before that, of how she had come to be there, but she rarely wondered about it in any case, only when she felt stifled a little as she did now, when she did not want them to know everywhere she was going.

The following morning she took her tray of buns and tarts and sold them all as quickly as she could, and then hiding her tray in a little crevice near a laneway, she set off, reaching Dorset Street as soon as she could. She went up the steps of the decrepit building and knocked on the chipped door. It was opened by an older woman who wore a frilly silky scarlet dressing-gown and had long grey hair blowing loosely about her. She had once been beautiful.

The woman looked her up and down.

"I wish to see Miss Mitchell." Bella said.

"She's gone out."

"Oh—when will she be back?"

"I don't know."

Bella felt deflated. She had not thought of this, and felt upset that she was unprepared as to what to do next.

"I say, if anytime you'd like to make a bit of extra money, I could find you—"

"No, thank you."

She hurried away without leaving her name. If Gracie heard that she had been discovered, she might up and go.

CHAPTER EIGHTEEN

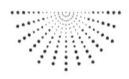

Philip received the letter into his hand, his heart beating with a mixture of joy and fear, for it was written in a girl's hand—his sister? He took it to the back of the bakery where he would not be disturbed and tore it open.

*Dear Pip*

*I write in a great haste, as I have to get this to you, I come to know Bella Coll is in great danger, from somebody paying a man to abduct and MURDER her, she is to be lured into a premises, I dont know anymore. I am fine and tell Ma I am fine give her my love and Julie & Ann too. I am not in Highgate anymore but no worry. Your sis Grace*

Philip felt his stomach turn somersaults when he read this. He looked at the clock. Bella was not back yet—he felt a rising anxiety, she didn't often go on the gad.

Mr. Coll was serving a customer. Should he tell him? Yes, he had a right to know—*no*—it would distress him and he could, with his weak heart, die on the spot—but his face gave him away, for he was ashen-faced and Mr. Coll was looking at him with concern as he gave the customer change.

"Is it your Ma?" asked Mr. Coll as understanding dawned in his eyes. "Go, as quick as you can, then."

There was no need to correct the assumption. There had been a few occasions when he had had to leave the shop for his mother's needs; he had never been sent a letter about it though, the message was always delivered by a young boy or girl from Jerome's Buildings, but Mr. Coll didn't wonder at it, which was a blessing.

It was only a short distance to the High Street and he reached Massey's Shop in minutes, and sprinted in.

"What do you want?" Mr. Massey demanded.

"Have you seen Miss Coll?"

"Miss Coll? You mean the one who tries to pinch my business? She ain't 'ere, why would she be 'ere? She never comes in 'ere, not that she wouldn't be welcome, if she was buying."

"This is urgent, man. Have you seen her today?"

"Well yes, she passed up this way this mornin' as usual, gave me a cheery wave, she did, but didn't stand outside, she went up the street a bit. 'Aven't seen 'er since. Is she orright?" He went on in a more concerned tone. "You better go and find her, afore she comes to any 'arm!"

Now Philip had to make enquiries among the businesses up along the street to find out who had seen her, or if they had noticed anything unusual.

Mrs. Cleary who sold potatoes from a barrow said she had seen her, but that she had finished up her business quicker than usual. Pete who sold old kettles and pots said he'd seen her turn into Old Castle, but he wasn't certain …

He felt desperate. He had to find Gracie and get more out of her about how she knew—it would lead him to the man with evil intent. But in his own mind, he knew there was only one man—or two perhaps—a father and son—who wanted to be rid of Isabella Coll.

Bella was walking in dejection around a corner on her way home, when she was almost knocked over.

"Owww! Look where you're going!" she said before she saw it was Philip. And a very relieved Philip at that.

"You're safe," he said, gripping her arms.

"Safe as houses! What's the matter with you? Knocking good people down, not like you!"

He hugged her, suddenly, and then drew back just as quickly.

"I'm sorry—I'm sorry—I'm just so relieved to see you in one piece, that's all!"

"Don't be sorry then," she said, secretly pleased. "Where are you off to, then?"

"I took it into my head to find Grace." He did not show her the letter, the word MURDER would frighten her to bits.

"I didn't tell your father where I was off to," he said awkwardly. "He thought I was going to see Ma."

"Oh, that's orright," she said. "I won't tell." Philip hoped that her father would forget that he had got a letter.

Philip was dejected too, to find out that Grace was out. There was no point in him continuing, so he turned to walk Bella home.

"You mustn't be lured in anywhere, you hear me?" he said to her sternly.

"Lured in anywhere, why are you warning me about being lured in?" she laughed at him.

"Oh, with all that's going on, murders and the like, it's just that I might worry about you."

"You have no need to worry about me, Philip, but—with all that's been happening, we have to find Grace and rescue her."

"We have to do that, but I don't know how," he said.

"I didn't leave her any message, in case it would frighten her away, but she might guess, if that—landlady or whoever she was—tells her someone was looking for her."

"I'll go back there in the afternoon." Philip said. "If you can cover the shop and close."

CHAPTER NINETEEN

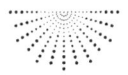

Bella was sweeping the outside of the shop that dark November evening of the inevitable litter it had accumulated during the day. Papers, apple cores, fruit peels, rags, a few empty beer bottles, and broken glass were all mixed in with the mud and dirt of the gutter. At least no donkey or horse had added to the mess today. Her father had gone up to bed early; her mother was getting supper. Philip had gone out at half past four.

She looked forward to going inside as she was hungry; the evening was turning cold, and she hadn't bothered to get her shawl. There was nobody on the street just now; she always had to wait until it was clear of carts so that she could take her broom out.

"Miss Coll! Miss Coll!" She heard a voice whispering her name with urgency. She looked up to see the smiling face of Mrs. Wilcox standing at Number 2.

"I have someone in here who wishes very much to see you," she said, beaming.

Someone to see her? That was astonishing. But—Gracie! It must be Gracie! Gracie, of course, would not want to show her face so near to her own home, but having heard that she was being looked for, and realising it must be Bella, she had contrived a way for them to meet. Poor Philip, sent on a wild goose chase while Gracie had slipped undetected into Lupin Lane!

She'd promised her mother she'd never 'darken the door' of this establishment, but this was different. She could not miss this chance to talk to Gracie and urge her to leave this dreadful life. Bella stood her broom against the wall and hurried towards Mrs. Wilcox. The older woman indicated she go inside first, and when she was in the hallway, she shut the door with a click and Bella heard the bolt shoot home. She whirled around in surprise. *Blimey, she locked me in!*—Mrs. Wilcox was not smiling now, but standing with her back to the door, looking at her with a small smile—Bella lunged forward to push the woman aside to free herself, but instead she was caught up in a pair of strong arms, felt a stinking breath on her face, and fell unconscious as a wad of cold, sodden cotton was pushed over her mouth and nose. Her last thought was of Philip's warning.

CHAPTER TWENTY

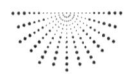

Philip was lucky this time. His sister was in, and agreed to see him. He went up to her room and stared at the floor when he realised what her activities there must be; she must have had the same thought and suggested they go for a walk.

"Don't—don't tell me about yourself if you don't want," he stammered. "This matter with Bella, you must tell me more—how you know—where you got the information. We can talk about other things later."

"I met a man in The Ten Bells. One of those braggarts that will tell you everything they ever did that was despicable and that they got away with.

This fool was approached by a toff, he called him, from Marylebone. He wanted him to do someone in for 10 pounds. This caused Mr. Mooney to laugh in his face. He wouldn't risk his neck, he said, for less than a hundred. Well, the toff wouldn't go for that, and made to go, so he brought it down to seventy-five. But Bert Mooney has no intention of risking 'is neck, so he asked around and found another fool who would do it, for twenty-five, a fellow they call The Crow, who I have met as well. So he is going on and on, and I ask him—and who is this poor person who is going to be done in, and he says it's a woman, a girl, who stands to inherit a business that was due to the man's son. So with Bella having relations in Marylebone, who we know don't like her, and all the rest, I got it out of him (he was very drunk) that she lived at Lupin Lane – that was enough, I knew it was Bella—then I had to find out how, and when—he said like I said in the letter, she'd be lured into a premesis, and then taken off to be drowned in the river, he said. But as to when—I had no luck at all."

"I did warn her," he said. "But I didn't mention the word murder—that would've frightened her."

"Well I think you should have, Pip. Bella will be tricked into going in someplace and maybe even by someone she knows—what's that place beside the bakery? That's a brothel, you know? Does she ever go in there? Cos I happen to know that The Crow goes in there and knows the landlady well."

CHAPTER TWENTY-ONE

"Where is Bella?" Nana Clancy was becoming anxious.

"She must have met someone out there and be caught talking. Come on we'll begin our supper, Mother."

But when Bella had failed to appear within ten minutes, it was time to go and see why she was delayed. Mrs. Coll was perturbed to find the broom standing against the wall, and not a sign of her daughter.

If she had known it, Bella was not one hundred feet away, lying on a bed in a tiny room upstairs at Number 2, unconscious. Her abductors were by turns looking out the window, and discussing the next plan.

"Remember, not a mark on 'er, so as to look like an accident, that she fell in," Mrs. Wilcox said.

"More's the pity, I like to get the job done quick, to be sure of it. But Bert said the guv'nor was most perticuler about drowning; the police have got all scientific, an' they can tell from scientific testing, how a person snuffs it. Even poison isn't safe to use no more."

"When's the cart coming?"

"Six o'clock."

"There will still be a lot of people around then. Somebody might see."

"Nah, he'll bring it right up to the door, if we put 'er in an old sack, she looks like potatoes."

"Why would I be sending out potatoes? Well never mind. Oh look, her mother's out in the Lane."

She can't be faraway, thought Sophie, looking at the broom. Should she alert Jim? There was no need to worry him yet, she thought. Where was Philip? He supped with them, too. Of course—he must have come by and asked her to go somewhere with him, she'd left the broom by and off she went—but without closing! That was careless. She was probably just around the corner, chatting to somebody after all.

She went in and locked the bakery and turned down the lamp. Bella would have to knock at the front door. At least she had done the till! She heard the sound of a cart going by, scraping the cobbles of the narrow lane. It appeared to stop outside her neighbour's establishment. She took no notice of the fact that it was late for a delivery.

Philip turned the corner from the High Street into Lupin Street just in time to see, through the archway, a cart heave away from Number 2 and turn the corner. What had a cart been doing there at this time of the evening? They got all their deliveries in the morning or at least in daylight hours. It looked suspicious. He ran to the bakery, but it was closed and dark. He banged the knocker on the street door of the house. Sophie came out.

"Is Bella here?" he asked quickly.

"No, she went out to sweep the lane, and went off somewhere—"

He exclaimed something, and took off, running.

"What is it, Philip?" she called out after him, but he was gone.

CHAPTER TWENTY-TWO

Philip ran as fast as he could, but already the cart was out of sight on the busy street. He felt sick at the thought that he would not be in time. The traffic moved briskly, but he kept pace. He passed a Hansom cab, somebody's fine carriage with insignia, a dustcart and finally caught up with one which he hoped was the one he had seen Lupin Lane. It looked like it carried some furniture, covered by canvas. Should he follow this? He had a stroke of luck—the driver turned around briefly, and Philip saw his profile. He recognised a man who often passed the bakery. Big, swarthy, collar turned up high. It must be The Crow. But he was not alone, there was a man sitting in the back with the goods.

But where was Bella? Tied hand and foot, gagged and terrified, hidden under a table? He followed, keeping his eyes peeled for a copper. But no constable in blue materialised. How long would it take the man sitting in the back to realise they were being followed? Off the busier streets, he managed to stay undetected by walking in the shadows.

They were getting closer to the River. He did not know how he was going to tackle both men and free Bella, but he would do it somehow. The cart trundled on, they were near to the Thames. London Bridge came into view. Giant warehouses and offices loomed above him.

The cart stopped. He hid in a doorway. London Bridge was very busy with vehicles and pedestrians; men and women thronged it, walking in all directions. Off to the side, under one of the ancient warehouses, was a downward path leading to the riverbank. The Crow hopped off his seat and led the nag down. Both men looked about them before taking the path; Philip tried to melt with the door.

He searched the faces of the passersby—was there any man he could enlist to help him? He would sound like a madman, gabbling about a woman being led to her death down this path. They'd laugh at him, and move on. But—he spied tall helmets bobbing in the crowd. Coldstream Guards! Four in number. He had no hesitation going up to them, addressing their officer. They not only believed him, but drew their bayonets as they prepared to march down the muddy path in the tracks of the cart.

"Hey there!" called the officer, shining his torch. "Halt!" Philip saw the men turn suddenly, and in the light he saw their eyes widen in alarm. They swore loudly before they leaped away in great fright and legged it toward the first pillar of the bridge, in among the grass and marshland, dodging behind boats lined up on the shore. Three of the men went after them—the officer stayed and shone a torch as Philip jumped on the cart and began to uncover the furniture. There was among them what looked like a sack of fruit or vegetables. Careful where he placed his hands, he found out that it was a human form inside, and so relieved was he to see Bella's face, streaked with dust and dirt, uncovered when he ripped open the top.

"Bella, Bella! Wake up!" he took her by the head and shoulders and shook her and at long last, she opened her eyes, raised her two arms, wound them about his neck, and began to sob.

CHAPTER TWENTY-THREE

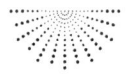

Bella wasn't physically hurt, and she recalled for him how she had been tricked, and the noxious smell of the man who pinioned her, and the feel of the cold, wet cotton on her face, and she was filled with horror at what would have happened to her if Philip had not followed the cart. She shivered with cold and fright. Philip gave her his jacket. He took her home. It was less than half an hour's walk. The Guards had not caught anyone, The Crow and his assistant must have known the area and were able to hide—even perhaps in the water—until the Guards gave up. They would have to make a report, they said, to their superior officer, but it was up to Miss Coll to alert the authorities that a crime had been committed against her.

Philip wished to go straight to the police; Bella was very reluctant. To do so would involve her Uncle Percy and Aunt Lydia; her father would be heartbroken.

"After all, I'm not certain he's behind it." she said.

"Who else could it be? A guv'nor from Marylebone? Of course it's him. Even though you're alive and well, he deserves Life with hard labour for plotting to do you in," said Philip hotly.

"We'll think of a way to punish them, without having my mother and father know they wanted to do away with me."

"What about Mrs. Wilcox? She led you into the trap."

"Why don't we call upon her now and see her face?" Bella's expression lit up. Philip wasn't sure he could see her face without doing some harm to it. She was determined in her plan, so before she went to her home, she knocked on the door of the establishment at Number 2.

The manservant answered, and Mrs. Wilcox came tripping out of an inner room. When she saw Bella, she put her hand to her head and had to support her frame against the wall.

"You're surprised, Mrs. Wilcox, I see. I was rescued by the Militia. The police may be coming for you any moment now."

"I didn't know—I didn't mean—it was just a joke—"

Bella turned smartly away. Philip had something to say to Mrs. Wilcox also.

"Get out of the East End." he said, wagging his forefinger in her face, and with as malevolent an expression as he could muster. "And take your friends with you. Know what I mean?"

Bella was received at home with relief. She had only been absent a little more than ninety minutes. She did not say a word about the danger she had been in. Her mother scolded her for going away like that, taking a walk just because she got the idea of walking around the shops, forgetting to close the bakery! The door wide open, and the takings where anybody could find them! A good thing her father didn't wake up! Bella endured the scolding bravely and bit her lip.

Her Nana was not so easily deceived, and looked at her with questions in her eyes.

## CHAPTER TWENTY-FOUR

It was Friday, and Bella, though she had not slept—even though there had been no noise at all next door—felt very shaken in a sort of delayed shock. But she forced herself to go out and sell. Around 11 a.m., a rumour swept down the High Street, causing stomach-churning horror and expressions of revulsion from shop to shop, from barrow to barrow, and stall to stall.

"What is it?" asked Bella anxiously.

"It's another murder. This time, in Spitalfields, on Dorset Street."

Bella became ashen with fright. Her first thought was for Gracie. She trembled all over. She had to let Philip know. She had a nauseated feeling. By the time she reached the bakery, she was of the opinion that it was not Gracie, simply because she wanted to believe that, and wanted to Philip to believe it, at least unless they found out otherwise.

Philip was rooted to the spot, his face white as the flour. "I have to go there, now."

"You won't get through, with all the coppers."

"I'll get as far as I can. Cover the shop, will you?"

He was back in a short time. To their relief, the unfortunate woman was not Gracie. But some poor unfortunate young woman had been killed, and somewhere, a family must be in the deepest grief.

"Perhaps this will make her see sense," Bella said with conviction. "If only she'd come back, I would ask Papa to write her a character reference, and she could begin again."

November wore on. Mrs. Wilcox disappeared and a FOR SALE sign appeared on her place of business. Nana Clancy was very pleased indeed, though Sophie and Jim wondered why their neighbour had not even bothered to tell them she was going. A procession of carts came one day and took everything away, and the two houses which had become one were now empty and lifeless. Lupin

Lane became a less busy place than it had been in years.

"Philip, I wish I knew something about where I come from," Bella said to him one day. "Do you think Mamma and Papa would be hurt if I asked them more about how they found me?"

"I don't know that, Bella," he replied with care. "Maybe they'll think you're restless and want to go away, or something. It's a delicate thing."

But Bella would not be moved.

"Ever since that night when they tried to—do me in—I've been wondering about who I really am. It would be awful to die, not having tried to find out."

"No hurry, Bella."

"Oh but there is. What about my natural father for instance? I know my first mother is dead—in my heart I know that—but what of my first father?"

Bella found the courage to ask her parents about this one evening as they were sitting by the fire after supper. They both grew a little quiet, and said that the only information they had had was what she had supplied them. Her first name, her age, and someone called Vovó. Bella was astonished. Vovó! Who could that be? She could not remember at all.

"You talked about a ship," said her father then. "Do you remember that now?"

Bella shook her head. "I don't remember any ship at all."

"And being made to eat figs and you got sick on somebody's best gown."

"Did I really?" she giggled, because it sounded funny, though she was sure it was not at all funny when it happened.

"You mentioned, once, a Captain White," said her father. "He was nice, he gave you sweeties."

Bella shook her head ruefully.

"I don't remember any of that," she said. "But—would you mind very much, if I were to try and find out more about myself?"

Her mother smoothed her apron with her hands; her father scratched the back of his neck.

"You will always be my parents, no matter what," she reassured them.

"It's orright, love, we understand the questions you must have—go and find out as much as you can, if you wish. But I don't want you going around parts of this city on your own!" her father said at last.

"I'll ask Philip to come with me wherever I go," she said. "We can do it outside shop hours."

Philip said that the Shipping Offices would be a good place to begin to find Captain White.

"White is such a common name!" exclaimed Bella.

"Lucky you are it wasn't Smith or Brown."

They visited the Shipping Offices, checked the lists, and found three Captain Whites alive and working from 1860 to 1874. One man was deceased, another lived in Southampton, another, who had worked for the East India Company, had retired to a boarding house in Canary Wharf. Bella drafted a careful letter, fearing all the time that nothing would come of it, and if it did, that she would be better off not knowing. She received a response by return, in an old copperplate hand, warm in tone, and inviting her to call upon him at 11 Fortnum Place, the following Sunday at three o'clock.

The house was a handsome building, sporting curtains at every window, and a stately red door. She and Philip, both in their Sunday Best, were soon climbing a staircase to the first floor and were received by the old gentleman himself. He had a weatherbeaten face under a shock of white hair and walked with a marked limp. He shook her hand, held it fast, and did she imagine it, or did a little tear come to his grey eye?

"Sit down, I will tell you what I know," he said, indicating two comfortable chairs in his parlour. The room looked out on the West End Docks, and seemed an extension of it in its décor. A ship's wheel on one wall, a sextant and other navigational instruments hung on another, an oil painting of a large clipper in full sail on a third, a map of the world on the fourth. They were offered tea, brought in by a Mrs. Culpeper, and over it, Captain White told a very strange story.

CHAPTER TWENTY-FIVE

*C*aptain White had been in command of the Srinagar, an Indiaman carrying passengers to the East Indies, or to whichever port of call they wished to disembark along the way.

*Standing on deck at embarkation time in Gravesend to watch the passengers come aboard, one day he noted among them, a woman and a little girl whom she carried. Seeing the passenger list, he knew that it must be Mrs. Woodston and her child Isabella Woodston. He welcomed them aboard.*

*She seems rather sad, he thought to himself. But what a beautiful woman, olive-skinned, with dark eyes, and shining black hair. She carries herself well. The child is a miniature of her.*

*"Mrs. Woodston, may I offer you a tour of the 'Srinagar'?" he asked her. "It isn't much different to other ships, but it does have a superior dining-room. I hope you will do me and my officers the pleasure of dining at my table this evening."*

*He saw the little girl crane her neck to see the masts.*

*"They're so high! Do they reach all the way up to Heaven?" she exclaimed, pointing.*

*Both adults laughed.*

*"Sometimes they touch the clouds," he answered merrily.*

*"I appreciate your offer, Captain, but I am sorry, I intend to eat dinner in my cabin. I am never separated from my child." Mrs. Woodston answered his question.*

*"Of course, of course!" Captain White felt a little silly, but wondered why she had not brought a nursemaid with her. She was not poor, but her clothes and trunks were not top-notch, either. "You may, you know, bring her to the dining room. There is no bar on children. It will be a change for both of you, for a cabin can get tedious."*

*"Very well, then, Captain," she beamed. "You will have to have good manners in the dining room, Isabella! This nice Captain White has invited us to sit at his table." The little one smiled so charmingly back at her. There was a very*

*close bond between mother and child, he could see, in the lingering gaze between them.*

*"You are going as far as Lisbon?" he asked her.*

*"Yes. I was born there. My family moved to England when I was a child. I married an Englishman, as you have guessed from the surname. Now I'm returning to Portugal to live. My husband will follow us as soon as his business in England is concluded." This last sentence was uttered in a lower tone of voice, and a shadow crossed her brow, and Captain White began to feel that all was not well, but was too much of a gentleman to enquire further.*

*The voyage was comfortable, the weather was good, and they encountered no storms. They put in to Lisbon at about midday one fine Monday.*

Captain White offered his guests more tea. Both were rapt at his story, and Bella's eyes were large and hungry for more.

"I don't remember any of that," she said faintly. The old man smiled at her with sympathy. He took a long draught of tea. His voice, when it began again, shook a little.

"We were to stay overnight in Lisbon, and everybody had shore leave. Lisbon is a busy port. Several other ships had come in before us, and the main Square—

Commercial Square—was thronged with people. There was—still is, I am sure—a famous sculpture there, of King Joseph the First, a hero to the Portuguese. It depicts him on a horse, in all his regalia, and at his feet, crawling about, are all the snakes whom he intends to vanquish. A rather impressive edifice."

Bella was listening intently. A sculpture … a statue … a man on a horse … something was taking shape in her memory, struggling to come to the fore.

"This part is an episode that is difficult to relate to you, Miss er Coll. I offered to accompany Mrs. Woodston and her child to view the sculpture, and she happily assented, and we walked through the crowd of people and finally got near enough to see it in detail. The child though, was a little wary of this large edifice, perhaps the snakes had caught her eye or something, but she did not like it. Her mother had let go her hand the better to point something out and a moment later a man dashed out of the crowd, to the child's side, picked her up, and carried her away. It was so fast that it was over before in the blink of an eye. The child screamed. The mother screamed. Several persons took off after the abductor. But he disappeared up one street, took another, the followers lost him, and he was not apprehended. Until I received your letter, child—I am sorry—Miss Coll—I never knew what happened to Isabella. Mrs. Woodston I put in the care of some friends I had in Lisbon, as I had to put to sea again the following day. She was in a very, very bad way. It was a most, most unfortunate occurrence, and I will never forget it. Unfortunately, I never sailed that route again, and retired after some months due to a bad leg, which you see before you—and I never found out what happened."

"I have always felt my mother died," Isabella said quietly. "But, can you remember if she had ever mentioned where she had lived in England?"

"Yes—somewhere outside London. A Heath. Thornton, or Hampstead, I do not remember."

"Hampstead Heath," Isabella said wonderingly. A fresh memory came to her—she tried to catch it— sunny days, singing in a church, fresh-smelling flowers!

"I remember it now." Isabella said as they walked away from Canary Wharf a short while later. "The man on the horse—the statue. I was frightened of him. Oh, Philip, I remember more! Being carried away, and hearing Mama calling my name over and over, but the sound getting fainter until it was gone altogether. I was carried to where a ship was docked, and this horrible woman—her name was Mrs. Petit—he handed me over to her and she took me on board. The next thing I remember is that she made me eat dried figs, and I vomited all over her gown, and she was very cross with me! She said: *"That's my best gown!"*

"Serve her right, then!"

"But what was I doing on a ship back to England?"

"I think it's time we looked for a Mr. Woodston, don't you? Where to begin? What about the East India Company?"

## CHAPTER TWENTY-SIX

They went to East India House on Leadenhall Street one afternoon the following week, there to examine the records of the passenger list of the *Srinagar* which sailed in April 1874 under Captain Edward White. There would hopefully be an address there for a Woodston in Hampstead. But there was not. The name Woodston was there, but the address given by the party who booked the passage was in Portman Square. He was a Mr. A. Woodston.

Bella felt her heart beat fast as they looked at it, and the clerk copied out the address for them. Philip was less pleased. Portman Square was *Gentry*. What was she going to find out? Did she know herself, how she might feel about the Colls, Lupin Lane, the Bakery,

Whitechapel? Toffs from Portman Square never even came to the East End.

Her parents were upset too, but like him, were brave and tried to hide it. Bella seemed to be drifting away in her head from all of them. Even her grandmother was concerned. What would happen, when Bella wrote to Portman Square? Would there be an answer? Would she be dreadfully disappointed if there was not? If her father had been living there all these years, and it was possible, had he looked for her? What of other family members? And had her mother really appeared to her from Heaven, as Isabella claimed, or had that message been the dream of a small child caught up in the wonder of Christmas Eve? These were anxieties that plagued them as Bella crafted the most important letter of her life in her little room upstairs. Most of all—when she found her own kin, would she be induced to leave them?

Business was brisk in the bakery when the letter from Portman Square was delivered. She tore it open. Philip lingered with a customer, half afraid to look around to see her face. Would it hold joy, or disappointment? He finally let the customer go and turned around. Her face had a glow.

"My father answered."

Philip winced at the appellation. Her father was the man now eating his kippers in the nearby room, not the stranger who had written her the letter!

"What does he say?"

"It is very short, in fact. Here it is."

*Dear Miss Coll*

*I received your letter of the 15$^{th}$ inst. Please do be so good as to call upon me at a time most suitable for you. I am home most evenings except Thursdays. Sincerely yours, etc, Alfred C Woodston.*

"Businesslike, innit?"

"I suppose so," she said, her eyes wandering about, as if not knowing what to make of it.

"So are you going to go, then?"

"I must, Philip. Will you come?"

"Me? Go to Portman Square?" he laughed.

"Please, Philip. I can't do it without you, I would be so afraid to face him."

"Afraid! But you don't remember him!"

"I'm not sure! I—think I might! But I'm confused. I remember living in the country, in a house with white walls. And I remember my mother there, and how we'd pick flowers in May—lilac—I can almost scent it! That's why I've always loved lilac, maybe! And a man used to visit now and then, a tall, stern man, and Mama used to cry after he left."

"Don't worry, Bella. I'll come with you." Philip knew that if Bella was going to put herself in a situation where she would be hurt, he wanted to be there. He didn't like the sound of this Papa.

## CHAPTER TWENTY-SEVEN

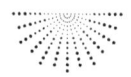

"You look beautiful!" Sophie said, blinking back the tears that came to her eyes when Bella came downstairs in her new coat, a coral pink with black bouclé collar, a row of black buttons down the front and a fetching black toque hat with a white feather, and black gloves.

"Mamma, please don't cry! I'm coming back!" Bella hugged her mother tightly.

"I know, dear, I know you are. I don't know why I'm feeling like this."

"Please don't worry, Mamma, it will be all right."

"Go and kiss your father and your Nana, then."

Bella embraced them warmly.

"I'm coming back in a few hours, you know," she said, shaking her head. "Where's Philip? Is he not here yet?"

As she spoke, he came in the front door, which had been left open for him. He was dressed in a good borrowed three-piece suit and sported a straw boater on his head. His shoes shone.

Bella felt perturbed. Her quest was troubling to everybody. Even Philip was uneasy. She knew he loved her. He had never said it; but he had no other girl. No news ever reached her that he had taken a girl out anywhere. He spent all his free time with her, except on his night off when he went to the pub with the lads.

"We'd better get a move on," said Philip. "After we get off the train we can go by hansom cab to Portman Square."

"A cab!" she said, astonished. "Why can't we walk?"

They saw her off at the door, waving. Now she felt afraid. Afraid that she was driving a wedge between them all, who had been so happy together always.

At last, they stood at the front door of Mr. Woodston's house. Neither had ever seen an entrance as grand as this.

"Spark any memories?" asked Philip. His hands were dug into his pockets, but he carried himself straight.

"Not at all."

The door opened. A middle-aged man stood there. Bella's heart spinned before she realised it must be the butler.

"We've come to see Mr. Woodston." she said.

"You are expected. Miss Coll and—?"

"Mr. Mitchell," said Philip.

"This way, please." The man led them through a carpeted hallway, with a mahogany table and a bronze sculpture of an Olympian athlete. A large mirror in an elaborate frame hung above.

They were being led upstairs. Old portraits looked down on them. Did they welcome them? Bella felt an increasing sense of dread with every step. She looked toward Philip with appeal in her dark eyes. He had been feeling nervous all day, but at the sight of her anxiety, he emboldened himself. He grasped her hand and gave her an enormous, encouraging wink, and mouthed something to her, she couldn't understand what it was, but it made her smile.

At last, they reached a white door and it opened, and they were announced. Miss Coll and Mr. Mitchell entered a large fancy drawing room in white and silver. A man with grey hair rose from his fireside chair and approached them. He wore a brown smoking jacket, which was too large for his spare frame.

He's much smaller than I remember, was Bella's first surprise. She searched his face—and could not find anything familiar there. She felt disappointed. Was this the right Mr. Woodston? He extended his hand and shook hers as if they had never met before.

"Please sit down," he said, formally, indicating two more chairs by the fire.

"May I offer you some refreshment?" he addressed Philip. "Some brandy perhaps?"

"Er—yes, thank you, sir." Philip was handed the smallest glass he had ever seen—everybody he knew drank tankards of beer—and was wondering at the mean-spiritedness of the gentry, until he took a gulp and the fire burned his mouth. Luckily his host was turned to Bella and asking her what she would like. She said 'sherry' as if it was the most natural thing in the world.

Philip learned that one sips brandy, and that he was careful to do thereafter. There was an awkward silence. He glanced at Bella; she seemed tense, sitting upright in her chair, not touching the back, her hands clasped tightly on her lap, clutching the sherry.

"I was very surprised to receive your letter, Isabella," said Mr. Woodston. "I had no expectation of ever seeing you again."

"So you are my father, then?" she asked eagerly.

"There is hardly any doubt. You are the image of your mother. God rest her soul."

"So she is dead, then."

"You knew that?"

"I knew that. But not how it happened."

"The entire story does not reflect well upon me." said her father. "And I suppose you want to know everything. Let me begin at the beginning. Your mother was the daughter of our Portuguese housekeeper, Mrs. Roderick. I became infatuated with her. Marriage to someone of lower rank would have been an anathema to my family, so when we married in secret in the late 1860's, I had to keep it from my mother. I was financially dependent upon her. I placed Maria—"

"Maria! Her name was Maria! I had forgotten!" Bella interjected.

"Yes, Maria Isabella. I rented a cottage for her in Hampstead, until such time as I wondered how to tell my relations and friends about her. You were born within a year. However, it soon became apparent to me that I had made a mistake—we had made a mistake—marrying."

"Why?"

"I had been infatuated, as I said. Such states do not last beyond a year or two. We had nothing in common."

Bella felt a cold rush of wind in her heart.

"You stopped loving her." she said flatly.

"I never really loved her. I am not proud of this, but such things happen. I tired of her, and of the pretense, of the obligation. The marriage and the secret became a burden. I wished to send her to Portugal where she had relatives, and thought her mother should go also. You must have met your grandmother. She went often to Hampstead."

A memory of a motherly older woman rose clearly before her.

"*Vovó!*" cried Bella. "Now I remember her—she used to visit us."

"That would be Portuguese for Grandmother. But to get on with my story—I wished to send her to Portugal where she had aunts and uncles etc, etc, you know. I wished however, to have you brought up here in England. I was going to send you to a boarding school. But I knew she would not leave without you."

"You didn't—you weren't—my kidnapper in Lisbon!"

"The young man—and the woman—were in my employ."

"That was—callous!"

"I see you have your mother's tongue. She used to berate me unmercifully about not acknowledging her."

"It was horrible, you don't know how I suffered, and she, too!"

"Listen to the rest of what I have to say, you have a right to know, though I would much rather leave it all where it was *before* I got your letter."

Philip silently uttered a word to himself, describing what he thought of this man, but was unable to say it in front of Bella.

"My man put you on a ship back to England, and the woman was to take care of you."

"Mrs. Petit. I got sick all over her dress, too, I did! She *made* me sick."

Her father waved his hands.

"I was doing what I thought was best. After you came back, you disappeared. I am sorry."

"I disappeared, just like that? And what happened to my mother?"

"She caught a fever in Lisbon, and died within a few weeks of arriving there."

"You killed her! As sure as if you had driven a dagger into her heart!"

He said nothing, only made another impatient gesture with his hands.

Bella got up to leave, and Philip rose with her. Her face was a portrait in anguish and disappointment. She turned around, and stopped dead in her tracks.

"I was here before," she exclaimed, pointing at the wall. "I was here in this room before!" she pointed to a gargoyle hanging there, an ugly object with lips open, snarling, and protruding eyes, which leered and grinned. "I remember that thing! I thought it was a monster!"

"I remember more," she cried. "I was brought here after I came back! I was brought up here by Mrs. Petit. There was an old woman here—your mother, was it? Thin, with a big white lace cap. She was not pleased to see me. I remember standing there on the carpet before her, and Mrs. Petit explaining that I was her granddaughter, and I was upset and I cried. You came in then. And I said *Papa!* That did it! She and you had a blazing row and I was crying my eyes out. I was taken downstairs—and to my great comfort, I was met by my *Vovó*! She looked after me and gave me a meal and put me into her own bed! And then next day, as I was sitting having my breakfast, a man came in and took me away again!"

"Mrs. Petit was incompetent. She was not supposed to have brought you here. She was supposed to have taken you to Abbeygate School for Girls. The following morning, I came downstairs to take you there, and Cook told me you had gone. I thought you'd run away. My mother's doing. She got rid of you, not I. What happened then?"

"I was put into a carriage, but I kicked and screamed and finally, he got tired of me and he put me out. I was on my own then. I must've run though all the streets of London before I ended up at Lupin Lane."

Mr. Woodston got up from his chair.

"I'm sorry you suffered at our hands, Isabella. I want, even at this late stage, to make it up to you. I never remarried. I live alone. You can, if you wish, come and take your rightful place here, as daughter of the House. I don't know how much education the Colls have been able to provide for you, but we can hire someone to teach you. I will provide you with enough money to dress yourself properly—" his eyes took her in from head to toe "—I can see you would benefit from that. I will be able to introduce you into society after you have gotten rid of that terrible Cockney accent. We can give it a trial, for, say, six months." He turned to Philip, the first glance since he had given him the brandy. "Mr. Mitchell, are you a cousin or—?"

"I'm her father's assistant, a Master Baker. Her *father* owns Coll's Bakery in Whitechapel."

"Very nice."

"Did you look for me?" asked Bella in an accusing tone.

"Well, of course! But London is a big place!"

"Where's Vovó now?" asked Bella suddenly, fearing the worst.

"My mother sacked her the morning after you arrived here. I do not know what became of her, I assume she returned to Portugal. I even thought that perhaps you both had gone to Portugal. Some of the older servants may know. There's an old retainer, Billings, I will ask him."

Billings was summoned. He was a very old man, upright, feeble, but he remembered Mrs. Roderick well. The last he had heard of her, she was in a house in Lambeth.

Bella left with her address, but with a hollow, deeply pained feeling about her natural father, and the amount of pain he had put her mother and herself through. He was a cold, callous man. She hated him. She would never go to live with him! Never! She was sure he hadn't looked very hard for her. If his mother objected so strongly, and he was dependent on her for everything, why would he want to find her? He didn't even look for her grandmother!

"Steady on," soothed Philip, though he was relieved for himself and for the Colls. "That's strong language, hate." He took her hand as they walked along.

Bella looked at the address she had been given.

"How far is it to Lambeth? Shall we go there, now?"

"Bella, I've got to see Ma today." Philip also had to return the suit to Bill Knowles, who was a salesman.

"Oh, of course. I'm being very selfish these days. You're so good to me, Pip, and I don't take it for granted, honest I don't."

"You should maybe think about the offer he made you," Philip said slowly. "Better yourself, you know? Maybe you should think about it."

Bella stopped dead in the street. "What, and destroy my parents? No way will I go to him!" she set off again quickly, ahead of him.

Philip did a leap in the air as he caught up with her.

## CHAPTER TWENTY-EIGHT

Bella was never so happy to walk into her old familiar hallway and greet her parents and grandmother in the living-room. She fairly burst in the door.

"It's good to be Home," she declared. "Home Sweet Home!"

It was all they needed to feel reassured. Over a cup of tea, she related everything that had passed.

"I want nothing from him. I hate him." she declared.

"Don't like that word 'hate' much," said her father. "He's to be pitied, I'd say."

"Why?" demanded Bella.

"Well, he doesn't have you, for one thing. He didn't have the joy of you. He sounds like a bitter old fellow, with a lot on his conscience."

"We'll have to pray for him, then." said Nana Clancy.

Bella stirred her tea slowly. She took out the piece of paper with her Vovó's name and address on it and showed it to them.

"May I be spared tomorrow, Papa? I know I can't take Philip away from work, so, Mamma, can you come? Please?"

Sophie agreed. She had nothing to fear now, and if Bella were to find out that her grandmother was dead, she would need her.

## CHAPTER TWENTY-NINE

Bella had never been to Lambeth before. It was a very old district in which Royalty had lived centuries ago. They stopped to look at an old red-brick Gatehouse, but it was not a time for sight-seeing, so they pressed on. Having asked directions twice, and gone astray more than once, they found Lambeth Walk, then Pedlar's Park, and going down a side street, they found Pedlar's Yard, a large, open area filled with people, sellers, stalls, and barrows, surrounded by decrepit, grim buildings with numerous windows, with washing hanging out of many. A few horses and carts stood about, waiting for nothing in particular.

"It's like Jerome's Buildings," said Bella, in dejection. "There must be hundreds of families here. Where to begin, Mamma? How do we find number 55?"

Sophie made an enquiry of a woman selling vegetables, and she pointed to a nearby door.

In the door, and up the narrow, cold staircase they went, which made Sophie very nervous, because there was no banister, so she stayed close to the wall side. Along a narrow, dank corridor they found the number they wanted, and knocked on the rickety door. It was opened by a middle-aged man, with hollow cheeks and eyes, clutching a coat around his emaciated frame. He coughed several times before answering their query.

"Mrs. Roderick? The Portuguese woman? She's gone. She went about ten days ago to the Union."

The *workhouse!* This was fearful news.

They were hungry, and stopped for a cup of tea and a bun at a teahouse. Bella's eyes were downcast.

"You will have to prepare yourself, luv, it might not be good news at the workhouse," said her mother gently.

They finished their sparse meal and having gotten directions, were soon at the sprawling building which dominated Renfrew Road. In the offices a short while later, Bella was overjoyed to find that Mrs. Bella Roderick, Aged & Infirm, was still alive.

They were shown to a dismal, overcrowded, stinking ward, where scores of old women lay in narrow beds, and Bella, her heart beating so loud in her chest she wondered if it could be heard, examined each ancient face one after another—for the attendant did not seem to know the names of all of the women in her care. After walking up and down twice, she became pessimistic.

"Take off your hat," her mother advised. "And let down your hair. Walk up and down again. And call her name!"

Bella did as advised. She shook out her long black hair and walked slowly between the row of beds. "Vovó? Vovó?"

At last, a quavering voice rang out in reply.

"I'm here! That's me!" The woman in the fourth bed was calling to her. She had long snow-white hair and a bony face, but her eyes were big and dark, and Bella, with leaping heart, knew she had found her Vovó.

"Could it be—could it be—little Isabella?" cried the old woman, raising two thin arms toward her. "For Maria is gone forever, my poor girl! It is Isabella!"

"Thank God she seems to be in her right mind." Sophie thought. All around her many of the women were staring at nothing, plucking at their sheets, mumbling to themselves. "Poor old dears!" she thought, and fear settled on her like a shroud. She sometimes wondered if the bakery would sustain Jim and her in their old age. If not, they too could end up in the workhouse. Without her mother's continued contributions down through the years, they would have found it very difficult, and might have gone bankrupt. Mrs. Clancy was getting infirm; she'd spent most of her money now. Jim was not healthy either. They had very little savings. Were they safe from an end like this?

"And who is this?" asked Mrs. Roderick, indicating Sophie, after a few moments of embracing Bella with tears and cries of joy from both.

Bella brought her mother forward to the bedside and put her arm about her with pride.

"This is Mrs. Coll. My mother. The very day I left Mr. Woodston's house, I ended up outside Coll's Bakery in Whitechapel. It was a dark, cold evening, and she and Mr. Coll took me in and cared for me and I have been with them since. They are my parents. My name is Coll."

Vovó caught Sophie's two hands in her own feathery, thin ones. Tears streamed down her cheeks.

"You took her in. God bless you and bless you! Such kindness, such wonderful Christian kindness! Look at her, such a fine, healthy, and beautiful girl! Such a warm smile, and her mother's hair."

"We were sent an angel!" said Sophie, crying now herself.

"Except when I'm stubborn." Bella flashed a mischievous smile.

"Ah, that is a family trait!" replied her grandmother. "Sit on the bed, for there are no chairs for visitors, and I will tell you what happened the last day I saw you, Isabella." She began to speak, stopping frequently for breath.

"When I sat you at the kitchen table to have breakfast that day in Portman Square, I was summoned upstairs to see Mrs. Woodston. She dismissed me there and then! When I came back down, you were gone! Cook had said she did not see you go, and the kitchenmaid said likewise. But I think they were lying, afraid to cross Mrs. Woodston. How could they not know? I packed my bags and left the house. No reference, just a week's wages. I was desperately worried about you. I went to Mr. Woodston's place of business—he's a Banker—and he said he did not know where you were—he had intended to put you in a boarding school. I went to the school—you had been enrolled—he was telling the truth. I went to the police. They said they would keep their eyes open but gave me little hope. So many children go missing in this City! I went to the workhouse, asked in shops, stalls, everywhere! I walked London! I couldn't find you! Finally, I had to get work, so I moved to Lambeth and took in sewing. And there I was, until ten days ago, and I had to come here, because my legs are weak now, and I have nobody to look after me."

"Dear Vovó, we will get you out of this place!" cried Bella, rashly, while Sophie looked a little concerned. She already had her own mother to care for, and Jim was frequently ill, how could she care for another person?

"It's time for us to go, Bella," she said. "We promised we'd be home before dark."

Bella opened her purse and took out two shillings and threepence, all she was carrying. "Please, Vovó, take this, you might be able to ask the attendant to get something that you need. I'll come back as soon as ever I can." She bent to the old lady, who grasped her head between her hands and kissed her forehead.

"So like your dear Mama!" she exclaimed.

"We must go," urged Sophie, and Bella left the ward, walking on air. This was only the second blood relation she had met in her life. The first was a great disappointment, but the second more than made up for that.

## CHAPTER THIRTY

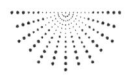

Philip was very pleased with her news. He wanted to meet Mrs. Roderick. Bella said they could go on Sunday. She wanted to bake her goodies and bring some little luxeries. She could not get her first grandmother out of her head; the initial joy was replaced with a fear that she had found her only to bid her goodbye, in death.

Philip had a mission to accomplish which he did not tell anybody about. Instead of taking supper with them after closing the bakery on Tuesday, he borrowed one of the new 'safety' bicycles from Alec Tupper, a mate who worked in a bicycle shop, and cycled all the way to Marylebone. Maybe someday I'll own a bike, he thought, as he whizzed through the traffic, between carts and hansoms and pedestrians, loudly ringing his bell. This wasn't like the penny-farthing, which could throw you over the handlebars.

He reached the Hardwicke house about seven o'clock.

Percy Hardwicke was living in fear of a knock on the door. The failure of the *Bakery Question* left him with mixed feelings. If it had succeeded, he'd have carried the stain of being a murderer all his life. He was remorseful. His great fear now though, was that Bella had gone to the police. He expected the police to call at any time.

And there it was, a knock. The manservant who answered the door was protesting loudly about something. He went out and saw that it was Philip and he was wheeling a bicycle into the hallway.

"I can't leave it outside, it'll be stolen," he was saying. "Hallo, Mr. Hardwicke."

"What do you want here?" Hardwicke said, angry and afraid. He was going to be blackmailed, that was it.

"Let him do what he wants with the infernal bicycle," snarled he, at the manservant, who walked away in umbrage.

"You know what I'm here about," said Philip. He felt very confident; he'd lost his awe of the gentry, or been cured of it. Or maybe he was still so angry at what had nearly happened to Bella that he just didn't care about Hardwicke.

"There's no point in denying it or beating about the bush. I have my sources," he continued. "You tried to murder Bella. I'm here to say one thing and one thing only. There are ships leaving for America everyday. You had better get yourself a ticket. One-way."

Strangely, that did not seem like a very bad idea to Hardwicke. He wondered how he had not thought of it himself! He'd have no fear in America. No police knock on the door. He'd get a job, with his accounting and legal experience. He'd slip away some morning soon, away from Lydia, having sold the house over her head. That would give him enough to live on for a time. She could go and plague Lucy.

"No—no police then?"

"Lucky for you, you old geezer, no police. Bella doesn't want to hurt her good father and mother. I'm of a different opinion, I'd like justice to be served.

We have solid witnesses; you could get Life with hard labour, if you didn't hang."

"So she isn't going to the police," Percy repeated, with relief.

"Not at the moment. She could see it in a different light if I persuaded her. But I prefer the ship solution."

"Very well then, the ship solution," Percy Hardwicke assented. "I will sail before the New Year."

"Make sure you do," Philip said, cramming his cap on his head and leaving the room. He took the bicycle and left the house.

"So were you going to leave me, Percy?" asked Lydia in a flat tone. She had heard everything. He did not reply.

"I am as guilty as you. I have no conscience, no heart. But I'm glad it was unsuccessful. I feel lost; my soul is empty. Why are they happy, and they have far less than we? Take me with you, Percy. We can make a new start."

Philip cycled steadily, stopping only for a quick cold pie from a cart, washed down by a mug of water. Not wanting to hand the bicycle back yet, he turned it towards the Bridge and looked out at the river. It was a dry, frosty night, and the moon was on the water. It looked nice. Romantic. He wished Bella were there to share it with him. He wished he were in a position to ask Bella to marry him. But he had little or no savings. He was blessed, though, to have a trade, and Bella never showed interest in any other man but him. But was he just her mate?

He thought of how he had just forced a wealthy bully out of England, and how easy that had been to do. But to declare himself to Bella—that would take another kind of courage. What if it spoiled the great friendship they had? What if she didn't think of him like that, and afterwards treated him differently? How could he continue to work in Coll's Bakery?

He hopped up on the bicycle again and sped through the dark streets. It was time to tell Bella how he felt about her, and if she did not feel the same, he would leave Coll's and become a Journeyman until he had enough saved to start his own bakery.

CHAPTER THIRTY-ONE

He had thought of a hundred ways to begin the conversation with Bella, but in the end used none of them. One day he left the bakery to walk her back from the High Street, and he dug his hands in his pockets in Lupin Street and casually said:

"I love you, Bella. You know that?" His heart pounded in his chest. It seemed like an eternity before she answered, but it was only two seconds.

"I know. I love you too, Pip." Her voice was tender and she had a rather silly look on her face, and he was sure he had the same on his.

"That's orright then," he said and they went on for about ten steps.

"When are we going to get married, then?" he asked.

"What about the New Year?"

"That's orright, then. I don't have money saved, but I'm a hard worker and I have a trade, thanks to your Papa. I'll have to do it proper and ask your father for your hand."

Neither remembered that she had two fathers; Mr. Woodston had seemed so little like one.

Mr. Coll gladly gave his consent, and bought a bottle of champagne to celebrate. Number 3 Lupin Lane had never seen champagne before, and the cork popped, causing their present cat to shoot under the sofa. They all laughed at Papa's drenched face and shirt-front. They drank the champagne out of cups.

"Bella, are you going to tell Mr. Woodston you're getting married?" asked Sophie quietly the following Sunday after supper. Philip was present, and they'd just eaten a good Shepherd's Pie prepared by Bella. Now they were finishing up with a slice of gooseberry tart with their tea.

"Oh no. There's no need for that. I want nothing to do with him." Bella snorted.

Her mother poured more tea, and her father spoke.

"You see, Bella, we think you should." he said in his quiet, firm voice.

"I don't want anything to do with him."

"Bella, your mother and I and Nana Clancy have talked about this. We think you shouldn't close yourself off from him."

"Why not? I was orright before I knew him; I'll be orright now, won't I?"

"There are a few things not so good here, Bella." Her father went on. "Firstly, this hate you have, it's wrong. Understandable, but wrong. He sounds like a bitter old man, and as I said before, to be pitied. You have to try to see him as Jesus sees him."

She was silent, but dug her spoon into her slice of tart.

"And then, there are the practical things. He wishes to help you get established in the world."

"And that is your due," chimed Mrs. Clancy.

"Maria would want it for you," said her mother.

"And, you could remove Vovó from the workhouse, and establish her in a place of her own, a good place where she would be cared for."

"She could maybe even move in with us," Philip said. He and Bella had decided on two rooms upstairs in the house that Mrs. Mitchell had moved to.

Bella toyed with her spoon.

"He owes it to Vovó," she conceded at last. "Turned out of the house like that by his mother! Maria's priest wrote to Vovó, and said that he had attended her in her last hours, and that she forgave Mr. Woodston. She knew it was him who took me. So, if Maria could forgive him, I suppose I can too."

Sophie lifted the teapot. "Anybody for another cup?" she asked, smiling.

There was a knock on the hall door, and Bella answered it. A delicate, fair figure in hat and coat stood outside.

"Gracie!" she cried in wonder and delight.

Gracie had been looking a little anxiously at her, but at her obvious welcome, and a warm hug, her expression turned to one of happiness.

"I'm out of that—life," she whispered. "For good. I met a wonderful woman, a Mrs. Butler, Josephine Butler, in a Temperance Hall—she helps women like me—oh, it's such a long story—I will tell you—again!

Does anybody know about me besides you and Philip?"

"Not a soul!"

"Thank you, Bella." Gracie squeezed her hand in gratitude.

It occurred to Bella then that she could also help Gracie make a new beginning.

Bella had a very unexpected surprise on Christmas Eve when she visited Lambeth workhouse. Vovó told her it was her birthday. She remembered well the first Christmas Eve with the Colls. Nobody had known it was her birthday, but she'd had a truly wonderful day.

CHAPTER THIRTY-TWO

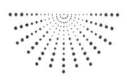

The wedding was a modest affair, but a very happy day for everybody who attended. Mr. Woodston had not been invited, but he did not appear to expect to be, and sent warm wishes. Gracie was bridesmaid. She had told Bella everything, especially what had happened to her when she was young, and how Mrs. Butler, who had been helping women like her for decades now, had told her that none of it was her fault, and that God was with her all the time, for He suffered at the hands of evil people also. "It's very possible that the woman taken in adultery, who Jesus saved, had had that happen to her too." was Gracie's opinion. Mr. Mooney, the man who had told her about the plot, had left the East End.

Mr. Woodston had written Bella a letter. He wished to buy her a wedding present. He also felt a gratitude to the Colls for raising his daughter, and giving her all the love and security that he had so miserably failed to provide. He wished to do something for them also. Bella felt emboldened. She discussed it with her parents. The larger house beside them was still for sale. Mr. Woodston bought it for her. Not only could she bring Vovó there, but Nana Clancy, who now found it difficult to manage stairs. Mrs. Mitchell wanted to come and live there too, and Gracie was very happy to accept the job of landlady and look after the old ladies. Mr. Woodston also began an Annuity for Bella, and of course, she was his only heir. Bella resolved she would go and see him a few times a year. She did not love him yet, but she was patient with herself.

The Hardwickes had sold up and gone to America, and it was a great surprise to everybody, except for Philip, but he kept that to himself, though Bella knew he had had a hand in it.

As the newlyweds danced together, Mr. and Mrs. Coll, dancing also, remembered the dark November evening they had found the frightened, hungry little girl outside their bakery. How beautiful she was now, how happy, and what a fine fellow Philip Mitchell was, the best they could have hoped for. They thanked God.

* * *

THANK YOU FOR CHOOSING A PUREREAD BOOK!

We hope you enjoyed the story, and as a way to thank you for choosing PureRead we'd like to send you this free book, and other fun reader rewards…

Click here for your free copy of Whitechapel Waif
**PureRead.com/victorian**

Thanks again for reading.
See you soon!

OUR GIFT TO YOU

AS A WAY TO SAY THANK YOU WE WOULD LOVE TO SEND YOU THIS BEAUTIFUL STORY FREE OF CHARGE.

Click here for your free copy of Whitechapel Waif

**PureRead.com/victorian**

At PureRead we publish books you can trust. Great tales without smut or swearing, but with all of the mystery and romance you expect from a great story.

Be the first to know when we release new books, take part in our fun competitions, and get surprise free books in your inbox by signing up to our free VIP Reader list.

As a thank you you'll receive a copy of Whitechapel Waif straight away in you inbox.

Click here for your free copy of Whitechapel Waif

**PureRead.com/victorian**

Printed in Great Britain
by Amazon